I0456908

ALL I WANT FOR CHRISTMAS
Michael Buzzelli

www.BOROUGHSPUBLISHINGGROUP.com

PUBLISHER'S NOTE: This is a work of fiction. Names, characters, places and incidents either are the product of the author's imagination or are used fictitiously. Any resemblance to actual events, locales, business establishments or persons, living or dead, is coincidental. Boroughs Publishing Group does not have any control over and does not assume responsibility for author or third-party websites, blogs or critiques or their content.

ALL I WANT FOR CHRISTMAS
Copyright © 2019 Michael Buzzelli

All rights reserved. Unless specifically noted, no part of this publication may be reproduced, scanned, stored in a retrieval system or transmitted in any form or by any means, electronic, mechanical, photocopying, recording, or otherwise, known or hereinafter invented, without the express written permission of Boroughs Publishing Group. The scanning, uploading and distribution of this book via the Internet or by any other means without the permission of Boroughs Publishing Group is illegal and punishable by law. Participation in the piracy of copyrighted materials violates the author's rights.

ISBN 978-1-951055-18-9

To Kelsey, the world's best Scottie dog

ACKNOWLEDGMENTS

Thank you to all my friends and family for all their encouragement and love. I am lucky to have a huge support system, and I am grateful to every single one of them. I'd especially like to thank those friends who bought multiple copies of my first book, and handed them out to their friends and family – people like Lonnie Janstch, Chuck Gilbert, Harry Caskey and Sandy Henry.

When my aunt, Terri Raymond, said, "You ought to write a Christmas book," I listened. This book is the result of that conversation. I couldn't have done it without her.

ALL I WANT FOR CHRISTMAS

Carousel

Kate watched the suitcases on the baggage carousel go around and around. Most of the passengers from flight 1581 had secured their bags, knapsacks, and overnight cases, hugged their loved ones, and headed out of Bradley International Airport in Hartford, Connecticut. She waited there a long while, but her beaten, brown suitcase was not invited to the luggage parade.

Thirty minutes earlier, hundreds of bags came streaming out of the conveyor's mouth. They would burst forth from behind strips of plastic, pushing the flaps aside. The luggage would flip and flop on the belt. The passengers of 1581 would greedily grab at the bags. Sometimes they would mistake one black suitcase for another. They'd check the tags and then return the cases back to the belt, where they completed their journey to their rightful owner. Some bags circled a few times before they were reunited. Kate kept a close watch for her own travel accoutrement, but the valise never showed up.

Soon, she stood alone, staring at the empty black belt, still chugging along without any bags circling on it. Now, only bits of ribbon, yarn, lint, a stray leather strap and a plastic GI Joe action figure trundled around on the conveyor. Kate watched the lonely soldier, dressed in camouflage fatigues, on his slow revolution around the belt.

Kate brushed back her hair and pulled a tattered envelope out of her coat pocket and checked her flight number on the printed ticket against the monitor above her. Right place. Right time. No luggage.

She walked over to the customer service desk with her ticket in hand. Hours earlier, she'd stuffed the envelope containing her tickets into the back pocket of her jeans as she boarded her flight. She pulled the envelope out again in Dallas where she ran across the terminal to catch her connecting flight. The envelope was mutilated after being folded and refolded endlessly.

A perky blonde service rep named Candace smiled at Kate even as she issued the bad news. Candace chirped, "Your luggage was accidentally rerouted to Miami."

Candace continued to smile and added, "We can get it back here on the morning flight."

Kate harrumphed. She muttered, "Great. Anyplace in the airport sell discount undies?"

Candace tilted her head like a confused cocker spaniel, and laughed, assuming that Kate was joking. The customer service representative smiled and spoke without any sarcasm. She issued a bright and cheery, "Merry Christmas."

Kate's natural instinct would have been to mock the woman, roll her eyes, or at least sigh in frustration. Instead, Kate simply turned and walked away, mumbling, "Happy holidays."

The large glass doors whooshed open and Kate stood outside in the brisk Connecticut air. A cloud of air billowed from her mouth and she could feel her nose hairs crystalize in the cold. When she left Los Angeles, it was seventy-nine degrees. Here, it was only nine degrees. She'd lost seventy degrees in transit.

Kate had a fleeting thought that she wanted to follow her suitcase to Florida.

***

In a rented blue Kia Sephia, Kate drove fifty-seven minutes to Bradbury, Connecticut, a charming, seaside hamlet with a town square complete with an amphitheater and a gazebo, quaint little shops that were usually spelled "shoppe," and a marina. Sailboats dotted the bay, but the water was a dark gray and the boats were abandoned, their colorful sails rolled up and bundled. Still, it was a welcome sight after the long journey.

Seeing the marina always made Kate joyous. Each boat was a landmark signifying that she had returned home. There was something about being back home in Connecticut at Christmastime. Connecticut was the quintessential Christmas state. Years ago,

Hollywood icon Barbara Stanwyck made a movie about it. Kate recollected jubilant family holidays. She felt long overdue for a perfect family Christmas.

After all, she was returning to her hometown as a moderately successful television comedy writer and she hoped to do a little bragging with some old friends and relatives, especially the ones who'd dismissed her when she announced that she was moving to Los Angeles after college. She couldn't wait to drop it into a conversation, particularly to Amy Norquist, a former high school cheerleader who was still working as a cashier in the A & P, eight miles out of town. Kate would have to make a special trip to rub her success in Norquist's face, but it would be worth it.

After graduating from Northwestern, Kate moved to LA. For four and a half years, she was a writer's assistant, a glorified gofer for a group of ABC sitcom writers. At night, she went to open mics and performed in an improv/sketch group on Melrose Avenue.

A few months ago, she leveled up to full-fledged comedy writer when her friend Matt Zimmerman offered her a gig on his show. Kate was a comedy writer for a new cable series, "The Matt Zimmerman Show." Even though Zimmerman wasn't such a great actor, and the ratings weren't very good, Kate was proud of her work on the show.

***

The brisk, wintry air was giving Kate a headache. She pulled over into the town square and ran inside the Ye Olde Apothecary Shoppe to buy a bottle of Tylenol. The pain reliever would have been cheaper at a Big Y, but the town had an ordinance about chain stores. The fact that there wasn't a big-box store within twenty miles was one of Bradbury's most charming characteristics.

The bracing cold, and the thought of facing her mother alone, gave Kate pre-migraine symptoms. Her brother had bailed to go on a Christmas cruise with his husband. While Drew and Connor cavorted around the Caribbean, she would have to make merry and bright with her mom. Alone. Drew was her buffer. It was her first Christmas without him since he was born, twenty-six years ago.

Virginia, Kate's mom, was the prototypical Connecticut mom. She managed a book club, volunteered at the library, and studied

Better Homes and Gardens and *Elle's Décor* magazines like they were her religion. She worshipped at the feet of the gods and goddesses of the Food Network, HGTV and Style networks. She was particularly fond of interior designer Patrick Mele, a local boy.

Virginia's marriage to Kate's dad, Glenn, ended seventeen years ago. Despite the fact that she hired a great attorney and got a massive amount of alimony, the two remained on good terms.

Glenn married a cocktail waitress named Cyndi and moved to Atlanta when he took the job of vice president of finance for a Fortune 500 cola company. Kate never took sides. While she tried to visit both parents equally, her mom always got the big holidays. Kate had scheduled an appointment on her calendar to call her father at five p.m. on Christmas Eve.

Kate drove up to her childhood home. It was a gray Victorian with a wraparound porch and white trim. The other houses on the street were bedecked in Christmas decorations, lights were strewn from gable to gable, and some of the neighbors had large inflatable figures in the front yard. Her mom's house had only one tiny, tasteful hint of Christmas. The front door was adorned with a Coastal Evergreen wreath, festooned with dried cranberries and a bright silver bow.

Kate punched in the garage door code and the gears hummed to life. The garage door rose. She parked and got out. She looked back at the car, remembering that she didn't have luggage, except for a small carry-on and her purse, and closed the door behind her with a press of a button.

At the bottom of the stairs, she yelled, "Ma?"

No answer.

She ascended the staircase from the rumpus room to the first floor. Again, she bellowed, "Ma?"

Finally, Virginia answered her call. "You're here?"

Kate looked down at her rumpled clothing, as if to check for certain that she was, indeed, where she said she was. Kate retorted, "Um. Yeah."

"I thought you were coming on a later flight."

That's how it's going to be, Kate thought. There was something accusatory in her mom's tone about her being early, as if she'd purposely given her mother the wrong information to throw her off kilter. Kate centered herself. She sighed. She was determined to make it a great holiday.

Kate marched up the stairs to the second floor. She explained, "No. I said I was going to take the later flight if the morning flight was overbooked. I wanted the miles and I wasn't..." She trailed off, and added under her breath, "...in a rush."

Kate walked into her mother's room and stared at her.

Virginia was packing a suitcase. Dresser drawers were open and clothes were flung around the room. It was chaos; an incongruity for her obsessive-compulsive mother.

"What are you doing?" Kate asked.

"We've been calling you."

"We?"

"Drew and I. You didn't answer. I thought it was because you were on a plane."

Kate realized that her phone charger was in her valise. She'd drained the battery on her flight listening to podcasts, playing Words with Friends, and skimming Facebook. The phone died somewhere over Albuquerque.

Kate clarified, "Phone needs to be charged. What's going on? Where are we going?"

"You know how Drew was going to surprise Connor with the cruise? Well, Connor can't get out of a big project at work. He can't go on the trip. He almost quit his job. Isn't that *crazy*?"

Kate plopped her carry-on and purse on her mom's bed and sat down beside them.

"I'm still not getting this."

"They wouldn't give Drew his money back. So, I'm going with him."

Kate was incredulous. She stammered, "Whatty what now?"

Virginia joked, "Did your ears pop on that plane?" Then she repeated, loudly, "I'm going on the cruise with your brother. I *told* your brother that he should have cleared the dates with Connor before buying the tickets. But, of course, my children don't listen to me."

"He got the lecture and he still invited you?"

"I told him it would be stupid not to go."

"Ma. What are you going to do on a gay cruise?"

Virginia was emphatic. "It's not a *gay* cruise. It's only a cruise."

Kate added, "With a lot of gay men."

Virginia looked puzzled, but continued to pack. She asked, "Really?"

Kate nodded. Drew must not have filled her in on all the specifics. It was a Christmas cruise for LGBTQ families. While it wasn't a raging gay party, it would be very festive.

"I plan on drinking margaritas and reading a book by the pool," Virginia said. "Maybe one of those boys will fix this mess." She played with her hair as she stared into a mirror on her dresser.

"I'm not sure, but I think that's borderline offensive. And margaritas? Ma. I don't know if you should be drinking again."

Virginia snapped, "Don't do that. It was a mistake."

Virginia unscrewed the lid on a mason jar filled with change. She started separating the quarters from the other coins.

"They have slot machines on the boat. I better take these."

She grabbed a handful of quarters and shoved them in a change purse next to her toiletry bag that was on her bed.

Kate said, "Ma. Slot machines have upgraded since you and Aunt Violet took that bus tour to Atlantic City. They take dollar bills now. Fives mostly."

"I'm taking a morning flight to Florida. The boat leaves from Miami in the afternoon. You have to take me to the airport tomorrow."

Three months ago, Virginia got a DUI on a ladies night out with some of "the girls" from work—all of "the girls" were over fifty. She'd rolled through a stop sign right in front of a police car sitting on the adjacent corner. It would be nine months before Virginia could drive again.

The word 'airport' reverberated in Kate's ears. She let out a sigh, as if air escaped her whole body. She tried to protest, saying, "I just came from the—"

Virginia caught the expression on her face and posited, "You don't want me to go?"

An alarm went off in Kate's head. She pictured the robot from *Lost in Space* flailing its arms about and screeching, "Danger, Will Robinson." She knew there was no right answer to her mother's query. If she said no, she was a killjoy. If she said yes, her mother would attack her for wanting to get rid of her.

It took the Wisdom of Solomon, but Kate said, "I want you to do… what you want to do."

Her mother beamed. "Great. I'm going on a cruise."

"A gay cruise."

Virginia shot Kate a look as she snapped her suitcase shut.

Kate had a sudden revelation: She would be alone for Christmas.

Her plans for a perfect Christmas were starting to fall apart.

Snickerdoodle

Kate took a long, hot shower. It felt good to get the airplane funk off her body. She stood in the shower as the warm water spilled down her back. Standing there in the shower, she admired her mom's soap collection. Virginia always kept a nice variety of fragrant, artisanal soaps in the metal shower caddy. Fancy soaps must be a prerequisite to be the quintessential Connecticut mom.

She used a bar that smelled of peppermint, a joyous scent of the holiday season. It reminded her of all the things she loved about Christmas.

Virginia cracked the bathroom door open and asked, "Do you need a toothbrush?"

Kate opened the shower curtain a few inches and squeezed her head out.

"Nope. I had my toiletries in my carry-on."

Kate resumed her shower, thought for a second, and popped her head out once more. "Do you have a spare eyelash curler and toenail clippers? The TSA guy confiscated mine."

Virginia pondered for a moment and said, "Yes. In the linen closet. I'll get them."

Kate bellowed, "Also powder."

Kate thought that if she was going to have to put on the same underwear after showering, she wanted a layer of baby powder between her body and the airplane undies.

***

When Kate was dressed—in the same exact clothes from before—she bounded down the steps and met up with her mother in the kitchen. She felt the warmth of the oven before she rounded the corner. The whole house was filled with the glorious aroma of cinnamon and spices, another joyous scent of the holiday.

Virginia was rolling out little white balls of dough and placing them on a cookie sheet.

"I was making snickerdoodles when your brother called, but I've been frantic ever since. Now that I'm packed, I pulled the batter out of the fridge and thought I'd finish them up."

Kate moved in close to assist.

Virginia sniffed her and said, "You smell like a baby."

"I used both Johnsons."

"What?"

"Johnson *and* Johnson? Never mind."

Kate rolled out cookie balls and placed them in a line on the tray.

"Did you make chocolate chips?"

Virginia nodded. "Yes. They're in the freezer. And thumbprints, pizzelles, tea-time tassies, four nut rolls, apricot horns, and those peanut butter cookies you like… the ones with the Hershey's Kisses in them."

Kate sang, "Two turtle doves and a partridge—in a pear tree."

Virginia scolded, "Don't make fun. I've been baking since Halloween." She added, "You're going to have to assemble some cookie trays and make some deliveries when I'm gone. I'll write a list."

Kate nodded. "What kind of phone do you have?"

Virginia pointed at her cell phone on the counter. "That kind."

Virginia had no idea about the make and model of her cell phone. Naturally. Kate picked up her mom's phone. It was dusted with a fine coat of flour. She wiped it off with a paper towel as she examined it.

"Damn."

Virginia stared at her. It was the sort of face any mother would make when her child swore for no seeming reason.

Kate explained, "I need to charge my phone. I'm going to have to buy a charger if my suitcase doesn't show up tomorrow. I'm guessing I'll have to buy some new clothes, too."

"You can go through some of my clothes," Virginia said. "I'm not taking any winter stuff with me."

Kate squirmed. She didn't want to be impolite, but her mom looked good in fall colors—tan, gold, and rust. Whereas Kate liked bright colors and bold patterns.

Her mother was quick to take the hint. "I think there's a box of some of your old clothes in the basement."

Kate yawned. "I'll check it out in the morning. I'm exhausted."

Eight hours on a plane with a layover in Dallas and the drive to Bradbury were beginning to take a toll. Kate could hardly keep her eyes open.

Virginia took two cookie trays out of the oven. The warmth enveloped them. She placed the hot cookies on a cooling rack, placed two more trays in the oven, and reset the oven timer.

Virginia swelled with pride and pronounced, "There." Her mother's eyes widened as if a light bulb brightened over her head. She exclaimed, "We should exchange gifts."

Virginia scrambled out of the kitchen and Kate followed.

The living room was immaculate. Even though it was spacious, it was sparsely decorated. A tall and elegant Christmas tree stood in one corner, a black, baby grand piano in the other. The tree and piano were separated by a large fireplace with a thick white mantel festooned with cedar evergreen garland. The whiff of pine from the tree and the garland were only slightly overwhelmed by the cinnamon scent emanating from the kitchen. The fragrances mixed well, producing a pleasant, Christmassy aroma.

A carved wooden Santa Claus stood by the fireplace. He was stretched out like a fun-house mirror version, tall and thin, slathered in a thin coat of burgundy paint so that his grainy wooden surface showed through. He was a shabby chic Santa.

Virginia picked up a beautifully wrapped present sitting under the tree. It was the size of a shirt box and was covered in a shimmering white paper adorned with a silver bow. Virginia handed the present to her daughter. Kate admired the time and effort that went into the impeccably wrapped gift.

She drew back the bow and unraveled it with methodical precision. She was careful as she picked apart the tape with the tip of her fingernail.

Her mother grew impatient. She ordered, "Just open it."

"It seems like such a waste to simply rip it open."

Kate tore at the corner of the box, ripping the paper off with one quick yank.

The box held a multitude of treasures. There were scented soaps, just like the kind she had been admiring moments ago: lavender, lemon verbena, cucumber and melon, and citrus aromas. One of the soaps, made with cinnamon and clove, reminded her of the cookies in the oven. The box also contained two lovely silk scarves: one turquoise and black, and the other a bright emerald green. There was also a pair of black leather gloves and a small envelope.

The Christmas card had a perplexed Santa with googly eyes on the cover. Inside it read, "I see you when you're sleeping." When Kate opened the card, two tickets to the Charity Christmas Ball and Toy Drive slid out.

"I bought a ticket for each of us. But you'll have to find someone to go with you. Maybe you can take Phil." She added, "I wonder if he has a tux."

Kate thought about taking her cousin to the biggest, most elegant event in Bradbury. She stated, "I'm guessing no, but I bet he has a dressy Starfleet uniform. The kind they wear when they meet the Vulcan ambassador."

Kate pictured her cousin Phil entering the grand ballroom at the hotel dressed in a blue tunic with pointy plastic ears glued over his real ears. It made her chuckle.

After her brief laugh, Virginia stared at Kate for a long moment. Finally, she said, "Well? Where's mine?"

Kate sunk her face into her chest as if her neck could no longer support her head.

She said, almost inaudibly, "If you're lucky, you can meet up with it in Miami."

Crickets and tumbleweeds.

Virginia asked, "Well, what was it?"

"A necklace. I got it from that cool jewelry store you like on the Third Street Promenade in Santa Monica."

"I love that place." Her mother brightened, and then the color left her again. She added, somewhat harshly, "You should put expensive items in your carry-on. *Not* in your suitcase. I swear. You would lose your head if it wasn't attached."

Their brief Christmas moment died a sudden death, pronounced dead three minutes after unwrapping the first gift of the holiday season.

Surprise

Tony had finished his third tour of duty in the Middle East and had successfully completed his mission: a covert operation in the desert. He was getting a rare treat. He was going to be stateside for the holidays and was overjoyed he'd get a chance to spend Christmas with his parents in Boston.

He thought he'd surprise them, until he saw an email from his dad. His father was the "Salesman of the Year" and won a trip for two to Hawaii. His parents, Frank and Maureen, were scheduled to fly off from their home in Boston one day before Tony's plane landed in the U.S.

During a long layover in Germany, he sat down at the Starbucks in the Berlin-Tegel Airport and video conferenced with his parents. He sipped a tall, caramel-colored coffee with two creams, no sugar in front of his open laptop.

His father beamed, "Salesman of the year, Tony. They don't give that out to just anybody."

Tony smiled and said, "Dad, that's great. Congratulations. You guys deserve a trip."

His father's smile widened, but, swiftly, the older man's face twisted. He appeared agitated.

"Spill it. I can tell this isn't a social call," his father commanded.

Tony ran his hand through his freshly shorn hair, and explained, "I've got some leave. I was going to come to Boston but now—"

His mother popped up in the background. She piped in, "You're coming home? If we knew you were coming back, we wouldn't go. Frank, we can't leave now. Is it too late to cancel? I won't go if Anthony is coming home."

His father spent some time trying to shush her, which only made things worse. He instantly regretted telling them.

"Look. I don't want your plans to go all FUBAR because of me. Go. Have a good time. I didn't know that my tour was over until twenty minutes before I was on the plane to Germany. Besides, I don't have a new assignment yet, which means I'll catch up with you guys after the New Year."

Maureen cried, "I'm so proud of you honey. So, so proud."

Tony didn't know if the cell phone camera could capture it, but he was blushing.

Frank asked, "Where you gonna go for the holidays?"

Maureen butted in, "Can you get a ticket to Maui? You can stay with us. I bet they'd let us put a cot in our room."

His father bellowed, "Mo, we're not doing that. Jesus Christ."

Maureen scolded, "Francis Alberto Rossi. Do not take the Lord's name in vain. Especially this close to his birthday."

Tony held his hand over his mouth so his parents couldn't see him laughing. His index finger bent upward around his nose up to his eyebrows.

"I'll figure it out. I'll probably go hang with Natalie and the kids."

Maureen smiled through the tears streaming down her face. "Oh. Your sister would love that. She could use some cheering up. This business with Dom..."

Frank bristled at the mere mention of the name. "Dom. Ugh. I never liked him."

His mother swatted his father on the arm. "Don't listen to him, Tony. He used to play golf with that louse every weekend they came to visit. Your father was fooled, like Natalie was. Everybody was. Everyone but me. I had an intuition." She turned to her husband and added, "Tell Tony about my intuition."

"Maureen, for God's sake, don't bore the kid with that shit." Frank looked back at Maureen, rolling his eyes before conceding and saying, "She had a dream that Dom was running in the marathon and disappeared before he got to the finish line."

She added, "Tell him about the sash."

His father said, "It's not a sash. It's a number. You know how they make you wear a number? Anyway, in the dream, all they found was his number right outside a port-o-potty, but the crapper was empty. Here's the deal, though, that dream was, like, two years ago, before he walked out on Natalie and the kids. Two freaking years. I say it doesn't count."

"Still." Maureen was insistent. "He didn't make it to the finish line. You see what I'm saying?" She gestured to "The Man Upstairs."

Tony said, "Look. I gotta jet. Literally. I'm gonna see if I can change my flight from Boston to Connecticut."

Maureen moved into the camera. Her face took up the entire screen.

"I love you so much, sweetie."

Turkey

At four in the morning, Virginia burst into the bedroom and announced, "We're late."

Kate lifted her head from the pillow and stared at her mother—almost as if she didn't recognize the woman in front of her. Kate was slowly waking up in the guest quarters—a room straight out of *Town & Country*. The nautical-themed space was illuminated by the soft blue glow of a lighthouse-shaped nightlight. The room had white wooden trim separating the two distinct colors of the room, navy and ivory, with the navy covering the bottom half portion, and the ivory covering the upper portion. Prints of tranquil beach scenes adorned the walls. Each photo had tufts of marram grass sprouting on the dunes, sun-dappled coastlines, and turquoise skies. Throw pillows with seashell prints on them were strategically placed all around. Before she fell asleep, she decided she'd call it the Captain's room.

Kate threw off the covers and sat on the edge of the bed.

Her mother said, "Good. You're up," and marched out of the room.

The rest of the morning was a blur. Kate gulped down a glass of orange juice and grabbed a half of a bagel for the road. They had to rush off to the airport. Even though the plane left at nine, Virginia wanted to be there by six-thirty.

It was a much quicker trip to the airport, with fewer cars on the 91. There was, however, some freshly fallen snow, less than an inch, but still enough to slow them down. The road was clear, but the hills were covered in a soft white blanket. There were a few patches on the steepest of slopes that gave way to the frosted green grass underneath.

After finally arriving, Kate left the car running in the White Zone as she pulled her mom's luggage out of the trunk. A heavyset baggage handler took the big suitcase and placed it on a cart.

Kate asked, "Do you have everything?"

Virginia clutched a small suitcase and said, "Yes. All my valuables are in my carry-on."

It was her mom's final jab at her before flying off on vacation. Kate made a conscious effort not to say anything sarcastic and hugged her mom instead. She managed to get an eye roll in while her face was buried in her mom's short, gray hair. The baggage handler noticed it and flashed her a wry smile.

After they disengaged from their hug, Virginia straightened Kate's turquoise and black scarf and gave her a kiss on the cheek. Kate was glad she threw her new scarf on at the last minute. She wore it proudly for her mother.

Virginia passed through the sliding glass doors and was gone.

Kate jumped in the car and drove to temporary parking. She decided to check on the fate of her own luggage since she was already at the airport.

At Baggage Claim, she waited twenty minutes before anyone came to help her. It was Candace. The blonde customer service representative spent a few minutes staring at the computer and reported, "I'm sorry, but your luggage was routed to Ankara."

"Ankara? Where is that?"

Candace frowned and said, "Turkey."

"Turkey?"

Candace nodded. "The country."

"Not the bird? Because I would hate it if my suitcase was stuffing for someone's Christmas dinner."

Sarcasm leaked out of Kate like air from a punctured car tire.

Candace merely glanced up at her as if she were speaking a foreign language and then returned to her computer. She made a few quick key strokes.

The blonde said, "Don't worry. I will take care of this. We will have it back in no time."

Candace's fingers flew over the keyboard.

"I'm getting it to London. From London we can get it to JFK—that's in New York—and get it here by late afternoon tomorrow."

Santa, Baby

When Tony was at the PX in Germany, he found a Santa costume on the rack. On a whim, he tried it on. He pulled the extra-large suit over his frame. He scrutinized his appearance in the mirror. The plush, red suit sagged on his military-tight body. The suit was constructed for a much larger man. He looked like the inflatable Santa in the Macy's Day Parade after most of the air was let out.

He chuckled to himself as he strapped on the bushy, white beard. Since he was planning a surprise visit home, he thought showing up in a Santa suit would make it even more fun. Originally, he'd planned to surprise his parents. Now that he was off to his sister Natalie's house, the idea seemed even better. He thought his young nieces would get a kick out of having Santa show up at their home unannounced.

He chose not to call, text, or e-mail Natalie that he was coming. He was anticipating the shock on his sister's face and the joy he would bring Danielle and Marie.

On the long flight, though, he had second thoughts. What if she wasn't spending Christmas in Connecticut? What if she went to see friends in Boston or decided to spend it with her in-laws—Dom was a shit, but his parents were good people.

Tony thought it through and chose to continue with his master plan. If things didn't work out, he'd take a train to New York and meet up with a few friends in the city.

Once he landed at the airport, he went to the men's room and changed into the costume. He even put on the snowy white beard, which fastened to his head with an elastic strap.

At baggage claim, he stood in the Santa suit watching for his luggage. The children at the airport would tug at their parents' sleeve and point. One small boy covered his mouth, overwhelmed by the idea that Santa was so close by. Tony smiled and gave the kid a thumbs-up. The child almost fainted.

Outside the airport, a cabbie named Ajeet picked Tony up at the taxi stand. The cab driver was a handsome, young Indian man with a bright blue turban. He turned back to Tony and asked, "Where to, my friend?" The cabbie added, "I must warn you, if you want to go all the way to the North Pole, it's extra." Ajeet laughed at his own joke.

Tony grinned as he searched the enormous pockets of the Santa suit for his phone. He had to look up Natalie's address. Once he found it in his contacts, he showed the phone to the cabbie. Ajeet made a few notations on a clipboard then punched the location into his GPS, nodded and said, "Yes. Yes. Good," and off they went.

After a few moments, Ajeet inquired, "Mr. Claus, what brings you to Connecticut?"

"I'm visiting for Christmas."

Ajeet cracked, "Isn't this your busy season?"

"I'm playing a joke on my sister and her kids. She doesn't know I'm coming."

"It's a shame I don't have reindeer pulling my cab. We could make a big show of it."

"Funny," Tony stated, but did not laugh.

Ajeet smiled. "I'm Hindu, but I love the all the American holidays." He added, almost to himself, "Everyone tips so generously this time of year."

They talked together for quite a while. Tony learned a lot about Ajeet and his family, and how hard it was to raise Hindu children in a public school at Christmastime.

"My children want all the stuff. Toys. Candy. The tree. My wife and I agreed that we would buy them some of the things. But we cannot tell my parents. My father would have a cow." Ajeet again roared with laughter at his own joke.

Since it was a long drive, Tony told him about his sister Natalie and how her husband Dom had decided one day that married life wasn't for him and fled for parts unknown. Natalie had to get a good lawyer and track him down so she could get child support.

It was easier to talk about Natalie. Tony had just come off a covert mission in a war-torn country and he had seen some pretty awful stuff. Discussing his confirmed kills didn't seem like a socially acceptable topic with his cab driver, especially while dressed as St. Nick.

***

At five p.m., Ajeet dropped Tony off on St. Catherine Street, right in front of Natalie's house. Tony thanked him for the pleasant ride and, true to the occasion, gave Ajeet a lavish tip. The cabbie smiled and said, "Ah. You really are the Santa Claus."

Tony dropped his duffle bag on the porch and knocked on the door.

Ten-year-old Danielle came to the door and opened it a crack.

Tony bellowed, in his best Santa voice, "Ho. Ho. Ho."

Danielle flung the door wide, and turned back and yelled up the stairs, "Mom. Uncle Tony is here."

Danielle was jubilant, but not fooled by his costume for one second. Thirty-two fifty on the Santa suit and he couldn't even trick one niece. Marie came running to the door. The girls were almost identical, though separated by two years. Their personalities were vastly different, however. Danielle was thoughtful and measured for a ten-year-old. Marie was wiry and rambunctious at eight.

Marie exclaimed, "Uncle Tony. Uncle Tony."

He didn't even fool Marie with his costume. He was two for two.

Both girls hugged him as tight as they could. They did not let go until Natalie came down the stairs.

Natalie was visibly flabbergasted. She stammered, "Geez. What are you— How are you— When did you?" She hugged him. It was a firm embrace. Natalie smiled and said, "You think you are wicked smart in that Santa suit, don'cha?"

Natalie had lived in Connecticut for twelve years but she still held tight to her Bostonian accent.

Tony smiled. "I'll explain everything."

Natalie snapped, "Not now. We're running late."

He said, "We are?"

She said, "Us." Natalie pointed at the kids. "I'm so glad you're here, but I wish you would have called. I have to drop off some lemon cakes at Margie's house—this pile of toys is for the toy drive—then we're getting hot cocoa and going to get the girls a picture with Santa Claus… um, the other one, in the park."

"That sounds great. I'll come too."

"Aren't you tired?"

"No. I'll come. Besides, the best way to get rid of jet lag is to adjust to the new time zone. I'll stay awake as long as I can."

Natalie smiled and said, "Perfect."

"Let me change."

"We're already late."

Tony realized he'd be stuck in the Santa suit a little while longer.

"Girls, go get Riley," Natalie ordered distractedly.

Tony inquired, "Riley?"

"Yeah. I got a new man in my life."

Tony heard a short, sharp bark as a square-jawed Scottish Terrier with coal black eyes strutted into the room. Natalie's husband was replaced with an adorable dog. Tony approved of the exchange. The dog took an instant liking to him.

Within seconds, Tony was back out on the porch with his sister, the girls, and the Scottie. He noticed that the mailbox was stuffed with cards and envelopes.

"Your mail."

Natalie had the leash in one hand and grabbed the mail with the other as they all walked to her car.

"And this one."

Tony handed her a big, fat manila envelope that she had missed.

It was the divorce papers. The marriage was officially dissolved. Tony watched as she read the news. The joy drained from her face.

It was going to take more than a cheap Santa suit to fix this Christmas.

Chance Encounter

On the way back from the airport, Kate found a Best Buy off the highway and bought a phone charger.

By afternoon, she had assembled seven cookie trays to deliver to friends and family. She studied the list and planned her route so she would end at her Aunt Violet's house, where she was expected for dinner.

Right before she left the house, she realized she'd forgotten to pull the charger out of the bag. She spent fifteen minutes trying to get it out of its plastic home. Finally, she grabbed a pair of scissors and tore into it. She plugged in the phone and realized she would have to set course without it.

Her first stop was Doctor Civitaresi, her mom's primary care physician. Every year, Virginia brought a cookie tray to Civitaresi, her nurses, and the technicians.

The doctor's office was in the town square. Because the streets were busy with last-minute shoppers, Kate had to park some distance from the medical building.

She marched down Front Street, carrying the tray with both hands. When the wind picked up, a sheet of red plastic wrap billowed up from the tray. At the corner of Front and Willoughby, Kate tried to tamp down the plastic wrap, while holding the tray against her stomach with one hand and adjusting the wrap with the other.

She heard a man yell, "Riley."

Suddenly a perky little black Scottish Terrier rounded the corner, the dog's pink tongue flapping back to the left side of his square face. The dog dragged his leash behind him. It caught on Kate's foot.

A man in a Santa suit, complete with a bushy, cottony beard, slammed into her as he rounded the corner. The tray of cookies hit her square in the face, and then went flying. Both Kate and the ersatz Santa fell to the ground with a resounding thud. She landed headfirst, but a snowy embankment cushioned her fall.

The Scottie circled back and started scarfing down the cookies that littered the street, chomping on pizzelles, thumbprints, and chocolate chip cookies in a matter of seconds. The dog huffed, taking a pause to breathe after gorging himself on the sugary street smorgasbord.

The Santa looked into a smashed empty coffee cup he was carrying and noticed that the beverage was splattered all over Kate. Her only clothes were ruined. Luckily, it was an iced caramel macchiato and not a hot beverage.

Kate got to her knees; she tried to gather up a few cookies and put them back on the tray, but they were soggy on the snowy ground. She realized it was an instinctive behavior. No one would eat street cookies, except the dog, that is, who was gobbling them up with unequivocal passion.

The Santa scolded the dog. "Riley. No!"

The dog looked up at him. Riley's chin was dotted with bits of cookie dough; a sticky pecan from a tea-time tassie was matted in his fur. The dog ignored him and resumed eating the cookies on the sidewalk.

The man in the Santa suit grabbed the dog by the collar, but the Scottie was still able to reach a few more cookies and a slice of a nut roll, swallowing it in one big gulp. The faux Santa clamped the dog's jaw shut. He repeated, "No. Riley. No."

The Scottie was giving the Santa serious side-eye, glaring at the man in the red suit. A soft growl emanated from his clamped mouth.

Kate looked at her clothes, her only clothes. They were *ruined*. Her fall to the curb had poked a hole in her pants at the knee and the shirt was doused with iced macchiato—though, somehow her new turquoise scarf was spared.

There was something else. She could feel the wind whistling through her mouth.

"What the—"

Kate reached into her mouth and felt the gaping hole in her front teeth.

"My toof."

The Santa smiled and said, "Are you okay?"

An attractive woman in her early thirties approached with two little girls trailing behind her. She looked down at the Santa Claus and sighed. Then she looked at Kate.

The woman scolded her, "Is that chocolate? You're not supposed to give him chocolate."

Kate looked up at her. "I didn't giff the dog anyfing. I'd be ffffuriousss with him if he wasn't ssso darn cute." She added, "I am—fffffine—by the way."

Without her front tooth, it was difficult to pronounce her S's or her F's.

Kate struggled to her feet as the Santa stood, too. He reached out his hand to her, but she was already upright. She waved off his attempt to help.

The Santa tucked the dog under his arm, close to his chest. He scratched his head with his free hand. The white pom-pom ball on the end of his plush red Santa hat bounced around with every movement of his fingers. The Santa said, "The dog kinda got away from me."

Kate nodded in agreement and said, "I see."

The woman unfurled the leash in her pocket and took the Scottie from the Santa's arms.

The Santa looked at Kate's mouth. He screwed up his face as if he had just bitten into a lemon. He peered into her mouth and said, "That looks bad."

"Fffff—" Kate noticed the two small girls standing nearby and did not complete her exclamation. Not that she could, at least, not properly.

She looked down at the debris that was once a gorgeous tray of cookies. Then, she stared at the snow-covered ground. "My toof's gotta be around here sssomewhere."

"We should look for it," Santa said.

Kate said, as best as she could, "It's a white toof in the sssnow. It won't be easy."

Nevertheless, Santa was on his hands and knees searching.

The woman secured the dog's leash. She made sure it was snug and let the animal back down on the ground. The dog pulled her toward the cookies splayed out in the snow, but she yanked him back. Finally, the woman said, "We have to go."

While on all fours, the Santa turned to the young woman and signaled that he needed another minute, holding up his index finger. Then, he pushed snow away with his hands. The Santa did not have any mittens and his slender fingers turned red while he searched. He found a walnut, a pecan, and a stray chocolate chip, but no tooth.

Kate touched his arm, signaling that it was going to be all right. She noted that this Santa had unusually large biceps under his red felt suit, as if he was concealing a grapefruit between his shoulder and elbow.

He said, "It's not in this section. How far could it have traveled?"

"It'sss cool," Kate said.

The Santa asked, "Miss, is there anything I can do?"

"Not unlesssss you're a denssstissst."

She couldn't say "dentist" or any letter S either, and she whistled and wheezed when she spoke, a result of the missing tooth. The Santa joked, "You sound like that gopher from Winnie the Pooh."

The little girls giggled.

Kate mimicked Samuel J. Gopher and said, "'Sssay, you ought to do sssomething about that ssspeech impediment, sssonny.'"

The two little girls howled with laughter; the littlest one covered her mouth and the older one held her sides. The Santa smiled broadly.

The other woman softened, taking pity on Kate. She pulled a business card from her purse.

"Dr. Schultheiss has evening hours. If you hurry, you can still catch him. He's in the Brightside Medical Building."

The woman pointed to the very building where Kate was headed. Though, she hoped that she didn't have to say the name Schultheiss out loud.

As Kate ran off toward the Brightside Medical Building, she turned and noticed that Santa was staring after her.

A Crowning Achievement

Kate stared at the registry in the lobby of the Brightside Medical Building. She found the listing for Herman Schultheiss, DDS. She smiled and fondly remembered the television classic, "Rudolph the Red Nosed Reindeer." The Rankin/Bass production had an elf named Hermie who wanted to be a dentist.

I just collided with Santa. I might as well have an elf for a dentist.

She stepped out of the elevator and wandered the halls until she found his office. She entered the cramped waiting room. It was the standard model waiting area, complete with a coat rack, a set of plastic chairs that linked together, and ancient magazines such as *US*, *People*, and *Time*.

The receptionist was a trim older woman. Her hair was wrapped in a tight bun at the top of her head. She had an imperious look on her face when she said, "Name?"

"Nolan. Kate Nolan. Ssssorry. I said that like a sssspy."

"You don't have an appointment."

"Yesss. I know. I have an emergenssssy."

"What is your 'emergency,' Miss Nolan?"

Kate pointed at her mouth. It took every ounce of civility to stop herself from saying, "D'uh."

The receptionist opened a sliding glass window and handed her a clipboard. The woman at the window was very concerned by the huge splotch of caramel macchiato on the front of Kate's shirt.

Kate caught her gawking at the splotch and said, "Pedestrian collision" as best as she could manage. Once again, the words came out mangled.

After Kate filled out the proper paperwork, the receptionist asked, "Miss Nolan, you checked this box that says you were referred by someone, but you left this space blank. Can I put down a name?" The receptionist pointed at the line on the paper and added, "For the referral."

Kate thought for a moment and said, "Put down Mrs. Clausss."

The receptionist stared at her for a long, uncomfortable time. Kate simply shrugged once more and said, "I don't know her name."

A few minutes later, another assistant ushered Kate back to see Doctor Schultheiss, sparing her any further judgment from the haughty receptionist.

Dr. Herman Schultheiss was no elf. The dentist was tall and handsome with shaggy blond hair. He had a sparkling clean white lab coat and lime green scrubs underneath.

The dentist turned to her and said, "What seems to be—"

Kate opened her mouth. He stopped in mid-sentence and exclaimed, "Whoa."

"I know. I look like the Wicked Queen in Snow White. You know, when she's in old lady drag."

The dentist stared at her for a long moment.

Kate added, "You know the part when she's peddling that poison apple? She's all 'Go on, have a bite, my pretty,' or whatever."

The dentist smiled as he patted his chair. Kate sat down in the caramel-colored dentist's chair. He slid a metal tray in front of her lap. The tray was filled with assorted gadgets, an explorer, a periodontal probe, dental pliers, and a multitude of sharp, pointy things. The dentist stuck a positioner in her mouth. It was a big plastic clamp.

Schultheiss said, "Bite down. Gently."

After placing a heavy lead vest on her chest, the dentist took a few x-rays, clicking a button from ten feet away.

He asked Kate a series of questions while he was examining her. Somehow, without her front tooth and with her mouth agape, he understood everything she said, even though she sounded like Chewbacca. The doctor was a loud talker. He had clearly gotten used to talking over the whir of the machines that hooked up to his dental chair.

"How did this happen?"

It didn't sound anything like, "I was on my way to deliver these cookies to Doctor Civitaresi when this dog came at me—" but he understood her nonetheless.

"You're Mrs. Nolan's daughter? You're Kate?"

She mumbled yes, even though his gloved fingers were deep in her mouth.

Kate said, "Owjuno," which meant, "How did you know?"

"Everyone in the building knows Virginia Nolan. She's legendary around here. When Susan—um, Doctor Civitaresi gets those cookies, we all go crazy. She shares them with my office and the podiatrist on the third floor. I like the ones that taste like tiny pecan pies."

Kate said, "Teeteetaffa," which meant "tea-time tassies."

Dr. Schultheiss said excitedly, "Yes. Don't tell any of my patients, but I secretly love sweets. Where are they? The cookies, I mean?"

She spat a mixture of blood and water into the funnel that whooshed away the crimson liquid. "The dog ate them."

The dentist was crestfallen.

He jammed his gloved fingers back in her mouth just as she said, "Mmememcah," which Dr. Schultheiss somehow knew meant, "There's more in the car."

He was ecstatic again.

***

After the x-rays developed, Dr. Schultheiss explained that the tooth, central incisor number nine, had a root canal and a crown several years ago. It was the crown that went missing, and the main reason there was no blood on the sidewalk when it flew out of her mouth. He would have been able to affix it if she had it with her. The tooth, however, was either lost on the corner of Front and Willoughby, or in the stomach of a voracious Scottish Terrier.

Kate reflected on the origin of the crown. She flashed back to a dodgeball incident in high school. She pictured the frightful memory in vivid detail. Amy Norquist had nailed her in the face with the ball, spilling blood all over the waxy gym floor. It brought forth a string of bad memories and, at that instant, she regretted being back in Connecticut.

Schultheiss said, "I understand you work in comedy."

Kate asked, "How did you know that?" but it came out as garbled as every other sentence she spoke since losing the tooth.

Schultheiss explained, "Your mother brags about you."

It was exhilarating learning that her mom boasted about her career. She felt empowered. It never occurred to her that her mother even acknowledged her profession, let alone bragged about her to the doctors in the Brightside Medical Building.

The dentist took his hands out of her mouth and walked over to the cabinets along the wall. He said, "Let's get an impression."

Kate responded, "I can do some funny accents, but I don't do impressions."

He deadpanned, "Impression... of your mouth."

Dr. Schultheiss plastered some pistachio-colored goo to her upper teeth. After a few minutes, it hardened. When he was sure the goo had solidified, he yanked it from her mouth. Kate was half convinced the rest of her upper teeth would be torn out, stuck to the green glob like bugs on a fly strip.

Before Dr. Schultheiss finished affixing the temporary crown in place, he had dismissed most of his staff. One lone dental hygienist named Francine stuck around to assist.

Soon, he adjusted the chair into an upright position. Francine removed a bib that was held on by roach clips.

Dr. Schultheiss was washing his hands at the sink when he said, "You're lucky. This is my last late night before Christmas."

He walked Kate to the reception area. They both watched as Francine put on her gloves and hat in preparation for the frigid weather outside.

Kate bent down at the waiting area and began writing a check for her co-pay when Schultheiss stopped her.

"You know, with the girls gone, I'm embarrassed to tell you this, but I don't even know what to do with that check." He added, "I'll have Betty call you tomorrow and get that all straightened out."

Kate unzipped her purse and put her checkbook away.

"Here, I'll walk out with you."

The dentist turned off the lights and locked the front door behind them.

"I have a wicked idea." he said. "You mentioned you had more of those cookies in the car. Do you think I can get some?"

Kate smiled. The temporary crown was a much brighter white than the rest of her teeth.

She said, without any imperfection in her voice, "Sure."

The dentist winced. "I should have the permanent crown in a few days. Because of the holidays there's only a slim chance I would get it before Christmas. Come back before New Year's Eve and I'll put it in."

"I am flying out on the twenty-seventh."

"I see." The dentist added, "I'll see if we can get a rush on that replacement. I don't like to leave my work for others."

Dr. Schultheiss walked Kate to the car. They had a pleasant time chatting as they strolled through town.

He asked, "Where is Virginia now?"

Kate said flatly, "Gay cruise."

The dentist was taken aback. "I didn't realize that she—"

Kate laughed.

"No. She's with my brother. He had this big plan to surprise his husband with a romantic trip but forgot to clear it with Connor first. He couldn't get the time off from work. So, Drew took my mom instead."

Kate imagined that Virginia was sailing into international waters on a ship full of Abercrombie models. She pictured shirtless men gyrating to syncopated rhythms. Then, she pictured her mother, holding a bottle of water, looking lost on the dance floor.

"Look, Miss Nolan—"

"Kate," she insisted.

"I was wondering—Kate—if you would want to have dinner tomorrow night. Since you're here on Christmas break by yourself."

She brushed aside a stray lock of hair from her face and said, "Um. Okay."

She opened her car door and the dentist moved in close. She wrapped her arms around him and gave him a hug. It was another awkward moment. As they disengaged from the embrace, Dr. Schultheiss pointed at the tray wrapped in plastic on her passenger seat.

He squirmed a minute and said, "I was going in for the cookies."

He looked down at his coat, probably to make sure none of the caramel macchiato splotch had gotten on his brown cashmere jacket, but the stain on her shirt was long dried.

Kate's cheeks reddened to a deep scarlet. She turned away from him, reached into the car, and handed him a tray of cookies. Of course, she thought, maybe she could blame her flushed face on the wintry air, instead of her deep-seated humiliation.

He looked down at the tray and said, "Oh."

There was a tone of disappointment in his voice. Kate gave him a sideways glance and

Dr. Schultheiss responded, "Your mom always throws a few red and green foil Hershey Kisses around. It gives the whole tray a real festive look."

Kate nodded, smiled, and replied, "I'll try that next time."

She got behind the wheel and waved one last time as the dentist walked away with the tray of cookies.

In the car, a few blocks later, she thought to herself, *Maybe it will be one of those weird meet-cute stories we can tell our grandchildren one day. "Kids, I met your pappy because I had a pedestrian collision with a dude dressed as Santa Claus."*

Kate laughed to herself. She was starting to feel optimistic about Christmas once more.

Santa Land

Tony walked around in the bustling town square with his sister and her girls. Natalie kept Riley's leash taut. Tony knew he wouldn't be given the leash again after the fiasco earlier.

When they got to Santa's Village, they saw several high school kids dressed as elves passing out candy canes to families waiting in line. There was a big sign that read "Santa will be right back," next to a golden throne on an elevated platform. The golden throne was nothing but an ornate wooden chair spray-painted with gold acrylic on a swatch of red carpet that was stapled to the stage. A Christmas tree stood tall and proud next to the stage. On the other side of the platform, there was a mailbox on a candy-cane striped pole. The mailbox had the words "Letters to Santa" in glittery red paint.

Tony, Natalie, and the girls joined the line.

Riley huffed, a sort of strange dog sneeze, and everyone in line turned around and noticed Tony in his Santa suit. He realized that it was a mistake to leave Natalie's house dressed as jolly old St. Nick. All eyes were on him.

One worker elf, a sixteen-year-old boy with a name tag on his elf costume that identified him as Sparkle-Bright Whizzywhig (his elf name), grabbed Tony by the hand. Sparkle-Bright announced, "He's back from the North Pole, everyone."

The crowd cheered.

Tony tried to pull away from Sparkle-Bright, but the young boy in the elf costume muttered to him through clenched teeth, "You're late."

Tony whispered, "You've got the wrong guy."

He retorted, "You see anyone else dressed like Santa Claus?"

Sparkle-Bright was a sarcastic little elf.

Tony scanned the crowd. Somewhere amidst the multitude, there was a guy shirking his job as Kris Kringle, but Tony couldn't get a bead on him.

Tony shrugged and said, "You got me there."

Sparkle-Bright pointed at the golden throne and commanded Tony to sit down. Unsure what to do next, Tony obeyed the sassy little elf and sat.

Sparkle-Bright announced, "Santa will see you now."

Natalie gave the leash to Danielle and said, "Hold him tight."

She tried to get close to Tony to stop him from doing anything foolish, but it was too late. A girl—with the elf name Raindrop Star-shine on her nametag—held Natalie back.

"Ma'am, everyone will get a chance to see Santa."

Tony stared at his sister across the courtyard. He could see the panic in his sister's eyes.

Natalie was horrified by the turn of events. Then, in a bizarre mood swing, her horror transformed into a fit of giggles. She covered her mouth and looked away from him. It was apparent she didn't want Tony to see her laugh. Except, for Tony, seeing Natalie chuckling at his situation reached him in a visceral way. It was good to see her smiling again. It reminded him of their childhood together. He always enjoyed making his older sis crack up. It was as if he were nine years old again, making silly faces at her in the pew at St. Stephen's when none of the adults were looking.

Tony decided there was only one thing left to do. He put on the pair of red mittens Sparkle-Bright had handed him and chose to be the best Santa he could be.

He bellowed, "Ho-ho-ho."

Sparkle-Bright took the next child in line and escorted him up to Tony. The elf placed the toddler on Tony's lap.

Tony glanced over to his sister. He watched as Natalie picked up Riley as if to show the dog the current spectacle. He noticed that she cradled the Scottie in her arms and nuzzled him, hiding her face behind the dog's pointy ears.

Then he saw the girls. Marie looked pained. She stared at him as if he had asked her to perform advanced algebraic equations. He saw the little one turn to her older sister and ask, her voice only just loud enough for him to make out, "I don't get this. Is Uncle Tony really Santa Claus?"

He smiled as Danielle burst into laughter. The girl bent over, holding her tummy. She laughed so hard she nearly fell down.

Tony relaxed once he noticed his nieces were enjoying his new role. He leaned back in the big, golden chair. He was unsure what he was supposed to do next. He adjusted the child on his lap. Sparkle-Bright moved in.

Sparkle-Bright turned his attention to the stunned child on Tony's lap.

"We're going to take your picture, okay? Why don't you tell Santa what you want for Christmas?"

The young pseudo-elf tilted the child's head toward Raindrop, who was adjusting a digital camera.

Tony bellowed, once more, "Ho-ho-ho. And what is your name, little one?"

He wasn't sure if the toddler was a boy or a girl. The child's lip began to quiver. Tony knew the kid was coming out of his stupor and was assessing the situation as dangerous.

The child's mother knew it, too. She shook a small teddy bear to get the toddler's attention and waved it around chaotically. The kid began to wail, screaming like a banshee.

Tony felt warm liquid dampen his left leg. The child was peeing on him, but he was determined to remain Santa-like and continue smiling.

Tony, in his best Santa voice, asked, "What would you like for Christmas?"

The child continued to yowl until the mother came by and snatched the kid from his lap. She quietly apologized while the kid kicked and screamed in her arms.

Raindrop turned to Sparkle-Bright and she shook her head. Sparkle-Bright tried to get the toddler back from the mother. There was only one steadfast rule at Santa-Land: No picture. No money. They had to get the shot. Even Tony knew that.

Sparkle-Bright managed to assist in calming the kid down, and promptly placed the child on Tony's right leg. Of course, the child peed on the other leg. Both legs were already wet from the earlier collision with the beautiful young lady and her tray of cookies. He had gotten the Santa suit wet when he was on his hands and knees, searching the snow for her lost tooth on the sidewalk. Thinking about the brunette stranger gave him temporary relief from his current situation. He smiled, which seemed odd under his current circumstances.

He looked down at the kid on his lap and continued to smile. In that brief second when the toddler was quiet, Raindrop managed to snap a few quick pictures. As soon as the shot was secured, Sparkle-Bright retrieved the child from Tony's lap and handed the kid off to the mother in a swift gesture.

The elf turned to him and said, "Are you ready to meet the next child, Santa?"

Tony nodded reluctantly.

That's when the other Santa showed up.

Picture This

It was almost nine-thirty when Kate pulled into Aunt Violet's driveway.

Violet greeted her at the door. It was uncanny how much her aunt looked like a younger version of her mother, Virginia. Violet had short silver hair like her sister, but had more rounded features.

Her aunt looked worried. "Oh my goodness. Are you okay?"

Violet hugged her on the porch and ushered her inside.

Kate began to explain. "I left my cell phone at Mom's and I couldn't call or text. I'm sorry I'm so late. You wouldn't believe it. It was a series of unfortunate events right up Lemony Snicket's alley."

As Kate removed her winter coat, she noticed the large portrait mirror in Violet's foyer. Kate scrutinized her own smile in the reflection. Her front tooth was not only whiter than the others; it was out of proportion with the rest of her teeth. The temporary tooth was a large, white square and did not match the rest of her mouth at all.

Kate said, "It looks like I decided to fill the empty space in my mouth by jamming a peppermint chicklet up there."

Violet took her coat and hung it on a coat rack. "I made a tray of lasagna. I know it's one of your favorites."

"I'm not allowed to eat yet. And I have a headache as it is. How late is Ye Olde Apothecary Shoppe open 'til?"

"Hmm. There's a pharmacy that's open all night, but it's twenty minutes away. Let me see if I have anything you can take. Maybe I have an extra-strength something or other."

Just as Violet disappeared up the stairs to the hall closet, Kate remembered the cookie tray in the car. She went back outside to retrieve it.

The women met up a minute later. Kate exchanged the cookie tray for some extra-strength ibuprofen. She gulped down two gel caps right in the foyer.

Violet winced. She said, "Sweetie, let me get some water."

Her aunt ran off to the kitchen.

A few minutes later, they were situated on the sofa, catching up. Kate dribbled the water when she drank it, a side effect of the Novocain that was wearing off. Violet merely smiled and continued a story about her grandchild, Dax. Violet scrolled through a myriad of pictures on her iPad, and Kate "oohed" and "awed" in all the appropriate places. The boy was adorable. He was almost two with a mop of blond hair and big brown eyes.

"Here he is with his favorite stuffed animal, a dinosaur he calls Blook."

"Blook?"

"He's not the easiest kid to understand. I think he's saying 'blook.'"

Kate tried to work out the puzzle. She blurted out, "That doesn't sound anything like Tyrannosaurus Rex."

Violet nodded in agreement.

Kate looked at the picture. Dax was snuggled in his big boy bed. Her old bed. The other day, Kate had learned that Dax was the recipient of her childhood bed. Her mother had donated the bed to him when the boy outgrew his crib.

"Gwen's almost got him potty-trained. Except—"

Kate inquired, "Except?"

"He wets the bed."

He wet my bed. Kate got oddly territorial about her old mattress and frame. She remembered she made out with Scott "Scooter" Thompson in that bed when she was seventeen. There were a lot of fond memories between those four posts.

"Gwen, Ed, and Dax were all here earlier for dinner. Phil came, too. We waited as long as we could, but we didn't hear from you."

Kate lowered her head. She explained about her luggage situation, including the basic bullet points about the cell phone charger.

Violet tapped her on her leg and chirped, "Oh. It's no big deal. You'll see them all on Christmas Eve. Gwen is having an open house. She's having some relatives, friends, and neighbors over to her new house on St. Catherine Street. Do you know where that is?" Kate thought for a minute, but Violet added, "I'll text you the address. It's going to be a big to-do. She's hired caterers and everything."

After a few more sips of water, the conversation shifted and Kate told her aunt Violet her story about the dog, the cookie tray, Santa, and the dentist. When she got to the part when Dr. Herman Schultheiss entered the picture, Violet gasped.

Violet bolted out of her chair and ran out of the room.

Kate stood up, unsure about the urgency of the moment.

"What? What is it?"

Soon, Violet returned with a local magazine, *In Bradbury*. The exclamation point was all in the tone.

Kate's aunt flipped through the pages of the local magazine until she got to the back section where the classifieds resided. She pointed at an advertisement.

"There."

Violet showed Kate a full-page ad with a picture of Herman Schultheiss, DDS. He looked especially handsome in his white lab coat, smiling out at the magazine readers.

Violet asked, "This Doctor Herman Schultheiss?"

Kate confirmed, "Yep. That's the one."

Violet sighed like a teenager in a local production of *Grease* and whispered, "He's dreamy."

Kate would have rolled her eyes if anyone else said it, but Violet could get away with corny like no one else.

Violet chortled. "I remember when this issue came in the mail. I have to admit; when I saw him, I wondered if he was single."

They both agreed that Herman Schultheiss, DDS was very good-looking. There was something about the ad that made her uneasy, though. It was a large picture of the dentist and didn't reveal much about the services he provided. Oddly, the advertisement on the opposite page was for a car dealership. The dealership used a large red flag as a symbol. Kate didn't see any irony at the time.

Duel

Tony waved to the other Santa across the courtyard. He was glad to relinquish his duties as Kris Kringle. He felt guilty, as if he were caught red-handed performing the other man's job, even though it wasn't his idea. In this case, he was literally caught red-handed, since Sparkle-Bright made him wear a pair of crimson mittens that belonged to the Other Santa.

Tony reminded himself that he did nothing wrong. He thought, *I was just following orders*, which instantly reminded him of the Nuremberg defense. Then he thought, *Befehl ist Befehl,* which loosely translated to "an order is an order." It made him squirm a bit as the other Santa ambled toward him.

The other Santa was much older than Tony. He looked more like a traditional St. Nick. He had a large belly—one that was mostly real fat and not padding. He was a much more professional-looking Santa Claus. His snowy white beard was held on by spirit gum and not an elastic band. He even had crinkly laugh lines around his eyes and a bald pate.

Sparkle-Bright's eyes grew wide. Seeing the two Santas together, the kid obviously realized his mistake. Tony and Sparkle-Bright made eye contact; the boy was pleading for forgiveness with the large, sad eyes of a Margaret Keane painting. Tony nodded at him to let him know it was okay, even though he was a little peeved that the teenager couldn't distinguish the obvious differences between him and the much older man.

Other Santa's face reddened at the sight of Tony standing in his place.

The older man boomed, "I knew it. They were trying to get rid of me."

It was clear that Other Santa was drunk. He slurred his words when he spoke. He threw his cigarette down and crushed it with the heel of his shiny black boot. Tony privately thought that an iconic symbol of Christmas should not have been caught smoking.

Tony rose from the makeshift throne. He was ready to relinquish his seat to its original owner. As the other Santa approached, Tony stepped aside to give the older man his chair, but the other Santa admonished him. He pointed at Tony with a crooked finger and hurled a string of expletives at him.

Tony looked around at the crowd, assessing the situation. He was mortified. There were children present, including his nieces, Danielle and Marie. He didn't need them to learn such crude language, especially from a foul-mouthed Santa Claus.

The words shocked parents and children alike. It was not the behavior the crowd expected from St. Nicholas, nor from one of his special helpers.

Other Santa didn't seem to care. He came over to Tony and sized him up. The two Santas stood nose to cherry nose. They bumped bellies; Tony's Styrofoam lining pushed up against the older man's bowlful of jelly.

Other Santa pushed Tony. The crowd booed and hissed. Tony stood his ground. He didn't want to fight back in front of the children. That, and Tony knew he could polish off the portly gentleman in a few precise moves. One swinging crescent kick to the older man's lower jaw would do the job.

Sparkle-Bright shouted, "We're going to take a short break folks. Santa has a visit from—um… his twin brother, Jiminy. Jiminy Claus."

Raindrop whispered, "Jiminy?"

Sparkle-Bright shot back, "It was the first name I could think of, okay?"

Unfortunately, the crowd did not disperse, it intensified. Dog-walkers and store patrons, who were merely strolling through the park or using it as a shortcut to get to the next shop, joined the crowd. Many of the teenagers held out their cell phones and began recording the incident. The air grew thick. Tony could feel the tension. There was a lull as Other Santa approached him, a quiet moment before the storm.

"Think you can get rid of me, do you?" Other Santa roared.

Tony raised his hands to his chest and held his palms out in an attempt to negate the older man's flaring temper. He shrugged and said, "I don't even want this gig."

Raindrop nudged Sparkle-Bright. The teenage elf moved in closer. He tried to separate the Santas, but the ornery older man pushed Sparkle-Bright aside. The boy's green-elf-hat-with-jingle-bells-on-top fell off. It made several tinkle-tinkle noises when it hit the hard, frozen ground. Sparkle-Bright's plastic pointy left ear was askew and on the verge of falling off.

Then, Other Santa jutted out his hands in an attempt to push him again, but Tony's instinct kicked in. He avoided the old man, dodging to the side. Unfortunately, the drunk Santa fell off the raised platform and smacked into the Christmas tree. He fell to the ground, taking the tree, the lights, and the ornaments down with him with a resounding crash. A red spun-glass ornament rolled out in a straight line for several yards before bouncing against an onlooker's tennis shoe and coming to a complete stop.

Other Santa rolled around on the ground, trying to free himself from the tree, but he became entangled in the string of colored lights before bursting forth from his multicolored shackles. The bulbs popped as he strained against them. Finally, he lay on the ground, free of restraint but exhausted. The fresh smell of Fraser fir wafted up into the air.

Tony jumped off the platform and extended his hand to help the elder Claus. Other Claus, however, shooed him away. The drunken St. Nick stood, albeit wobbly.

"I'm sorry. This got out of hand," Tony explained, smiling in an attempt to diffuse the matter at hand.

Other Santa was unrepentant. The old man lunged at Tony, but, once again, the nimble Navy SEAL dodged out of the way. Other Santa slammed into the mailbox that read "Letters to the North Pole."

The tin mailbox broke free of the candy-cane-striped pole. The mailbox fell on the man's foot with a thud. Cards and letters poured out, all addressed to Santa Claus, mostly written in crayon. Tony noticed Sparkle-Bright mouthing the word "Ouch" as the older St. Nick hopped around, releasing another string of expletives.

"I think he broke a toe," Sparkle-Bright said to Raindrop.

"Which one?"

"Does it *matter*?" Sparkle-Bright shot back at her.

After a few moments of hopping around like a lunatic, Other Santa returned his focus to Tony. The drunk in the red Santa suit limped up on the platform to confront him once more.

Sparkle-Bright ran back into the fray. The teenage boy got up and stood between them, but Other Santa pushed the kid down on the throne. The pointy left ear finally detached and fell to the ground.

Raindrop ran over to Sparkle-Bright's side. "Should we do something?"

"Call nine one-one," Tony ordered both elves.

The girl reached for her phone and started dialing.

Tony knew that if he hit the old drunkard, he could possibly kill him. He tried very hard to defend himself without striking back at his opponent. Other Santa grabbed him by his arms and they began to struggle. They grappled with one another.

He heard a tiny voice in the crowd. "Which one is Uncle Tony?"

"I'm not sure, sweetie. I'm not sure."

Tony reached his limit when the old man tried—unsuccessfully—to knee him in the groin. He couldn't take it any longer and punched the not-so-jolly elf in the face. Other Santa fell off the riser. He was unconscious before he landed. Luckily, the padded red suit cushioned his fall.

The man was out cold, splayed out on the raised, red-carpeted platform. Teenagers in the crowd continued to record the action on their phones.

Tony looked out at the crowd apologetically.

Sparkle-Bright and Raindrop tended to the unconscious Claus.

During the commotion, he finally found Natalie. Her jaw dropped, as if the muscles in her mouth decided to stop working. Tony looked over at his nieces; both Danielle and Marie looked confused. The girls had watched their uncle beat up Santa Claus—possibly the real one—and they were horrified. Even Riley began to bark.

His training kicked in and Tony took control of the situation. He simply walked through the crowd, gathered his family, and calmly walked out of Santa's Village.

Natalie protested, "But—"

She turned back to see the commotion on the stage, but Tony commanded, "Just keep moving."

They heard sirens in the background. Tony didn't want to be there when the police showed up. He had a sterling reputation to protect.

By the time they got back to Natalie's house, viral videos went halfway around the world. The video was titled "Santa on Santa action: The Claus are out."

The video showed up on the local eleven o'clock news.

Hello Kitty

The next morning, Kate got up at seven and ransacked the boxes in the garage, looking for something to wear. The boxes were not marked. She found two of her brother's tennis trophies, a Fisher-Price playset, one broken Rock 'Em, Sock 'Em robot, a silver thimble and a race car—but no game of Monopoly to go with them—and a lot of dirt, dust, and cobwebs before she opened the box that housed her old sweaters. The box was incorrectly marked "kitchen appliances" from an earlier move.

She found a yellow Hello Kitty sweatshirt from ninth grade and tried it on. She looked at herself in the mirror in the rumpus room. It fit. But it was still a yellow Hello Kitty sweatshirt.

She stared into the mirror and said out loud to her reflection, "This is why no one liked you in high school."

Sadly, it was one of the few garments in the box that fit her. In a separate box she found a pair of jeans that also fit. They were snug, but they would work.

She was stuck with ancient apparel until she could get to the mall. Unfortunately, she had a lot to do before she could buy new clothes. Kate had to take the remaining four cookie trays out of the car and divide the cookies up so that four trays became six. After all, she'd spilled one, and gave Dr. Schultheiss the other.

She found the bag of Hershey Kisses and sprinkled them on the trays. The dentist was right. It made the cookie trays more attractive, festive. Though it started to irk her that he was brash enough to mention it.

Around eight, she called the airport. After waiting on hold for twenty-five minutes, she found her suitcase was not where it was supposed to be. *Big surprise*. Her luggage had been rerouted to Athens, Greece. The customer service rep explained that they identified her bags and would get them to Rome, then to the US. They would be sent to Kennedy, then Hartford. After all that, she was assured someone would deliver them to the house.

With her suitcase out exploring the world, Kate realized she had to buy clothes and some new Christmas presents for her Aunt Violet, her cousins Phil and Gwen, Gwen's husband, Ed, and their son, Dax.

She was hoping to replicate the presents she'd already bought, because it would be too hard to think of brand new gifts to buy them.

It was December twenty-second, and buying Christmas gifts this late in the game wasn't going to be easy. Still, she knew if she planned the day well, she could get it all done and be back in plenty of time to get ready for her date with the dentist.

***

Kate unplugged the phone from the charger and listened to her phone messages. There were several from Drew and Virginia notifying her about the change in Christmas plans. Old news. There was one from Virginia where she mentioned she arrived safely in Miami and was boarding the boat. Before she got to the last call (Aunt Violet wondering where she was), there was a series of calls from work.

Her assistant said, "Call me back when you get this."

The head writer, Doug McGeever said, "We need to talk ASAP." He actually said "asap" as one word and not the letters. No one was saying anything and she started to panic.

It was John Elias Hartnell, producer of *The Matt Zimmerman Show*, who broke the news to her.

Hartnell said, "I don't want to ruin your holiday vacation, but the network canned us."

"We're canceled?"

"Yeah. The ratings just weren't there."

Kate knew that cancelation was inevitable. She could sense it coming, like someone with a broken bone could sense a storm brewing.

The Matt Zimmerman Show had only aired three episodes before its demise. Last week's *Hollywood Reporter* wrote, "Not every rising new comedian should get his own show. Zimmerman is walking proof." *Entertainment Weekly* gave the show a C-, and the *TV Guide* gave it a Jeer, practically an obituary for a new show. Most of the critics had liked the writing, but not the acting. Matt Zimmerman, who was really funny in person, couldn't act—though that hadn't stopped any other comedians before him. Now, the first job she ever loved was gone. She felt bile churn in the pit of her stomach.

Kate spoke with Doug a bit longer, but no new information was added. He wasn't able to answer any of her follow-up questions, such as "Do I have to clean out my desk?" and "Will I be let in when I come back from my trip?" and "Is my health insurance still good?"

Hartnell said, "You should be fine with your WGA insurance. As for the rest, there are a few people in the office today. If I learn anything more, I'll update you, but you know… the studio is a ghost town during the holidays."

Her hopes of a perfect Christmas were finally dashed. No clothes. No job. No front tooth. She said, out loud to no one, "This Christmas is *literally* the worst."

Babe in Toyland

From deep slumber, Tony heard someone yelling his name. Slowly, he opened his eyes and saw Natalie standing next to the bed.

Natalie continued shouting his name. He was groggy, jet-lagged. He looked up at her and then put the covers over his head and rolled over. Natalie shook him. He turned back and looked up from underneath the covers.

His sister said, "You're on the news."

He bolted upright, awake.

She said, "I was brushing my teeth and standing in front of *Today*. I wanted to catch the weather, when this woman—the one with the wavy brown hair—I don't remember her name. Anyway, she mentioned, 'A bizarre incident in Bradbury, Connecticut caught on film.' Then, they cut to somebody's cell phone video of you and that Santa Claus fighting in the park."

Tony got up, threw on his terrycloth robe, and cinched the sash as he ran downstairs. Natalie followed him. Their haste caused Riley to scramble after them. The dog barked at them as they stood in front of the television. Natalie was able to muzzle the dog as they waited for the commercial break to end.

After a lighthearted ad for fabric softener, a tedious commercial for a diabetes medication, and a promo for a new episode of evening drama, the morning show returned. Tony and Natalie watched the dueling Santas fight in the town square. They flipped around the channels. It was on *Good Morning, America*, *Today*, and a couple of cable news networks. One cable outlet played the video every twenty minutes, right after news, traffic, and weather.

Natalie continued to flip from network to network. She glanced over at Tony and said, "This is not normal."

He merely nodded in agreement. His jaw was slack, his mouth agape.

***

Three and a half hours later, Tony bit into an apple while he watched Natalie brush Marie's hair. The girl would buck and whine whenever the brush hit a tangle. She gently put her left hand on the girl's shoulder to hold her in place.

Natalie commanded, "Hold still." She glanced at the clock as she combed out the knots in her daughter's hair. "Can you do me a favor?" she asked.

Between bites, Tony muttered, "What do you need?"

"I'm taking the girls down the street. One of their friends is having a Christmas party. We left a box for the toy drive in the garage. Can you take it down to them?"

"Sure."

"Keys are on a hook in the kitchen, next to the Advent calendar."

Tony turned to leave.

Natalie turned back to him and said, "Tony." She gave him a smile and tapped her fingers against her leg. "I know I haven't said it yet, but I'm glad you're here."

He looked back at her, winked and disappeared into the kitchen. Tony grabbed the keys and punched out the last two days on the Advent calendar. Christmas was fast approaching. He donned a big puffy ski jacket that used to belong to Natalie's husband, Dominic, and went out the back door. He got a little lost on the way to the warehouse, having only been there once before. He had assumed he'd remember the way, especially since they had been there last night, but he missed a turn. While it was very cold out, the sun was shining and the sky was bright blue. At one point, he pulled over and took off the bulky ski jacket. The puffy sleeves were cumbersome while driving.

He finally arrived at the back door. He didn't bother putting his coat back on because he was only planning on running in. He grabbed the box and jogged to the back door. The door was ajar and he butted it open with his shoulder while holding the box firmly in his hands.

Tony called out, "Hello?"

No one answered. A sixty-year-old woman with stark white hair finally entered the room. She smiled at him.

"Hi. I'm Natalie's brother. She wanted me to drop these off."

"You were here yesterday? Dressed as Santa?" The woman didn't wait for an answer and instead simply turned to the open door in the back and yelled, "Beryl. Get out here. You have to meet Natalie's brother."

Tony looked around and shuffled his feet. Several cardboard boxes sat on pallets, all filled with toys

"Stay right there," she said. "Put the box anywhere."

Tony set the box down as the woman's friend, another sixty-year-old woman with dyed red hair, came into the room.

The woman said, "This is Natalie's brother."

The other woman said, "I'm Beryl. This is Claire."

Claire moved in close. She touched his arm.

"Beryl. Feel that. It's like a rock."

Beryl moved in and touched his arm. Tony decided to show off a bit and flex. He used to be a scrawny kid before he joined the military. With long hours and hard work, he'd grown into his muscular frame. Too much attention, however, made him blush.

"You were Santa yesterday," Beryl said matter-of-factly.

"Yep."

Claire turned to Beryl and said, "He doesn't look anything like Santa now."

Tony backed up. His day was slipping away from him.

"So, I really just came by to drop off the toys." He pointed to the box he'd brought.

Beryl said, "Wait. Wait." Beryl pulled an envelope out of her back pocket. She continued, "I was meaning to give this to Natalie. It's two tickets to the Christmas Ball."

Tony took the envelope. "Really?"

"Yes. I was supposed to give it to her yesterday, but it completely slipped my mind. Please. She earned it. She did so many hours of volunteering down here."

"I'll tell her," Tony said. "My sister could use a night out."

"There are two tickets. You should come too." Beryl winked at him.

"I'll probably stay home and babysit. Someone's gotta stay with the girls."

Claire whispered to Beryl, "He's like Cinderella. But he's a boy. A really, really handsome boy." Even though she said it under her breath, Tony could hear every word. He blushed again.

"I bet we could find a babysitter." Beryl was insistent. "I have a granddaughter who could do it."

Claire touched his stomach. She said, "Beryl. Beryl. Feel this."

Beryl touched his tight tummy. "He's all ripple-y."

Tony couldn't help but smile at the completely inappropriate little old ladies. "I do a lot of stomach crunches."

Claire snickered. "He's better than Johnny Thunder from the All Male Revue that played down at the Jefferson Music Hall. And he was something."

Tony's face was as red as yesterday's Santa suit.

Malled

Kate ended up at the North Coast Mall a few miles from town. It was jammed with shoppers, but she had to buy a new batch of presents since it seemed pretty likely that her suitcase was not going to make an appearance before Christmas.

She circled the parking lot like a vulture scanning for a dead carcass in the Mojave. She drove the car very slowly down the lane, following a woman who was walking to her car. The woman was loaded down with bags and was clearly annoyed that Kate was stalking her. She finally turned to her and said, "I'm not leaving. I'm sticking these in the trunk and going back in."

Kate rolled down the window and was going to say something snarky, but thought better of it. Then she saw brake lights flip on and she raced down the aisle to grab the spot from an SUV that was pulling out. The SUV drove off and Kate whipped her rental into the parking space. A husky woman in a yellow Jeep stopped right in front of her.

When Kate got out of the car, the woman in the Jeep got out.

The husky woman barked, "That was my spot."

Kate simply stared at the husky woman.

The woman snarled at her. "I was coming the other way and I saw the spot. It's my spot." She moved closer to Kate.

Kate looked around, hoping for witnesses in case the situation turned ugly. She saw a young man walking toward them and let out a little sigh.

Husky Woman repeated, "That was my spot."

The young man got closer. He pulled his keys out of his coat pocket and hit the button. The doors of a blue Honda in the same row unlocked with a beep, and Kate turned to the young man and asked, "Are you leaving?"

He nodded. Kate turned back to Husky Woman and said, "He's leaving. Take his spot."

"That's not the point. That's my spot."

"I'm not gonna move, not if this guy is gonna leave. Just take this one." She pointed at the young man's car.

The woman scowled said, "Don't be flip with me."

The young man hovered by the door of his car, watching them argue. Kate looked over at him and said, "Can you please just go?"

He stared at her and then back at the angry, husky woman. Husky Woman was about to pop a vein in her forehead. Her face was beet red. The young man shrugged, unlocked his car door, and got in. He pulled out of his parking space very slowly.

"Please. Can you just take this one?"

"Bitch. You gotta problem with me?"

"No. I just don't understand this. Go here."

Kate motioned again at the parking space as the young man drove off.

"Would you—"

Kate pointed at the now empty spot and tried to guide the husky woman in as if she were landing a plane.

The husky woman walked over to her and came inches away from her face.

"Are you making fun of me?"

"Look. Someone else is going to pull in here if you don't."

The husky woman looked at her, then she looked at the spot. A line of cars was forming behind the yellow Jeep. Any minute now, someone would swerve around it and park in the space. Kate knew that if anyone else parked there, she was a dead woman.

The husky woman weighed her options quickly and said, "I'm pulling in. But stay here. I'm not done with you yet."

As soon as the husky woman got in the yellow Jeep, Kate darted out of the parking lot, weaving between parked cars, so the husky woman in the yellow Jeep wouldn't try to run her over.

Kate was out of breath by the time she made it to the shopping mall. That's when she realized the husky woman probably keyed her rental or slashed her tires. She thanked her lucky stars that she paid extra for the insurance.

Kate knew about the Christmas curse. People were nuts at the mall from Black Friday until New Year's Eve. That's why she always shopped early and did most of it online.

She cursed the airlines again for losing her luggage.

***

The mall doors whooshed open and she stepped inside. Once she was inside, her winter coat felt heavy on her body. The temperature at the mall was 80 degrees on the inside. Gobs of sweat poured down from her forehead.

She took off her hat and gloves and shoved them in her coat pockets. She unzipped the jacket and tried to air out the sweat. After running through the parking lot, she was hot, sweaty, and gross.

That's when she ran into Amy Norquist.

Amy beamed. "Oh my gosh. Why it's little Kate Nolan. I can't believe it. The big-shot comedy writer from my old high school."

Amy was with an older woman who was not her mother. They were both impeccably dressed. The older woman was very smartly attired, like a senior model from J. Jill, Coldwater Creek, or Talbot's. Her hair was blonde, but with only a tasteful touch of gray. Amy turned to the older woman and said, "And can you stand it? She can still fit into her Hello Kitty sweatshirt from high school."

Kate closed her jacket as if a cold wind blew through the mall. "We went to high school together?"

Even though she would recognize Amy Norquist anywhere, she tried to feign indifference.

"Kate, it's me. Amy Norquist. Norquist for now, at least. I want you to meet my future mother-in-law, Deborah Billingsly."

"Please, call me Deb," the older woman said.

"Mother-in-law?"

Amy blurted, "I'm engaged. You probably didn't get the alumni newsletter. No one can keep track of you now that you're living in Hollywood."

Kate queried, "We have an alumni newsletter? From high school? Who knew?"

"Of course. You'll have to give me your Hollywood address and we'll get you on the list. That way you can keep up with all the *important* people." Amy turned to Deb and said, "Can you believe it? She lives in Hollywood, California. Like a movie star."

Kate said, "Actually, I'm in Los Feliz. It's sort of…Hollywood adjacent."

"Los Feliz. That sounds so…ethnic. Is that a good neighborhood?"

Amy whispered "good" as if it were a dirty word.

Kate said, "It's lovely, actually. I'm on Hillhurst. Near the library."

Kate realized that specific directions about her neighborhood were meaningless to Amy. It was like describing chartreuse to someone who was color blind.

Amy smiled with clenched teeth and said, "You always did love…books." She whispered "books" as if it were also a dirty word.

Kate merely smiled back, even though she wanted to slap Amy.

Amy looked terrified when she noticed Kate's smile. There was a long moment of silence. That's when Kate realized that Amy and Deb were both staring at the chicklet. Kate got flustered, knowing the bright, white square was now garnering all the attention.

"My tooth. Yeah. It's temporary. I lost my crown."

Amy turned to Deb and said, "Speaking of crowns, I was just telling Deb that I kept my tiara and sash from when I was Homecoming Queen. I was just saying that when I walk down the aisle, I'm going to need something blue. You know… something borrowed, something blue? I thought it'd be a real stitch if I wore my blue sash from high school. You remember the big blue sash saying 'Homecoming Queen'? Wouldn't it be hilarious if I wore that on my wedding dress? Can you imagine a bride wearing her Homecoming Queen sash from high school? Oh. You should use that in your little routine, or on that comedy show you write." Amy turned to Deb and added, "She writes for a TV show. It's called *The Mike Zipperman Show*. She's like a celebrity. Almost."

Kate said, "Matt Zimmerman. It's *The Matt Zimmerman Show*."

Amy laughed. She knew she was getting to her.

Deb smiled and said, "I think I've heard of that," but added, "I don't watch much television, dear."

"Welp," Kate said after another awkward pause, "I better get going. I have a lot of shopping to do."

"My God. You still have Christmas shopping to do?"

Amy turned to Deb and said, "She used to be early for everything. My goodness. Look how things have turned around." Amy pivoted back to Kate and said, "Why, we wouldn't have been in here at all today, but we scheduled an appointment with the photographer on the second floor. Chuck and I have to get an engagement photo for the *Gazette*. Otherwise, we wouldn't have come to the mall at all. Ha. I rhymed."

It took all her acting skills to continue smiling at Amy Norquist and her soon-to-be-mother-in-law. Kate pictured Meryl Streep handing over her Academy Awards and saying, *"You simply must have them, dear. I'm no longer worthy."*

Deb looked back at Kate and added, "Chuck is my son."

"I guessed that. I'm a good guesser."

"Amy said you were funny."

"Amy," Kate said sweetly, "that's so nice. You were bragging about me to your new family?"

Amy said through her clenched smile, "Don't you know you're like a local celebrity around here? The funny girl… you were always the funny one. You're the funny girl who made it in Hollywood—er—Los Feliz…wherever that is." Once again, Amy whispered "Los Feliz," pronouncing it "Los Feee-lez."

Amy's cell phone rang. She pulled it out of her purse and showed Kate the screen, as a picture popped up. It was a photo of a handsome man on a tennis court, holding his racquet and smiling.

"Speak of the devil. It's Chuck now. This is him. Isn't he a-freaking-dorable?"

He was stunningly good-looking. Broad-shouldered, blond, with perfect teeth.

Kate used the opportunity to bug out of the conversation. She whispered to Deb, "Nice meeting you."

Deb smiled back. As Amy moved away to take her call, Deb followed.

Kate walked away, waving. She heard Amy say into the phone, "You will not guess who I just ran into. Oh. You wouldn't know her. Everyone made her out to be some big, successful muckety-muck living in Hollywood. She doesn't even live in Hollywood. It sounds like she lives in some Mexican border town. Yes. Mexico borders there. Somewhere. I don't know, honey. I hope you're not marrying me for my geography skills."

She and Deb howled with laughter. Kate assumed that Chuck was laughing, too.

Just then, the husky woman from the parking lot sauntered into the mall. Kate ran over to the playground area in the center of the mall's vast courtyard and hid underneath a green plastic sliding board shaped like a frog.

Kate crouched down low. She was ruminating on her encounter with Amy Norquist. It hadn't gone as planned. Kate was caught in her Hello Kitty sweatshirt, with her glaringly obvious fake tooth. Worse, *Entertainment Tonight*, TMZ, and *Extra* were most likely running stories about the cancelation of *The Matt Zimmerman Show* later that evening. Everyone in town would know that "Kate Nolan: Little Miss Hollywood" was a fraud.

She was at her lowest ebb, hiding from a husky woman under the kiddie slide at the mall.

Comic Relief

Kate tried on several fancy cocktail dresses at Nordstrom's. The salesgirl talked to her in short, clipped sentences, until Kate whipped out her credit card and bought a cute cocktail dress in basic black.

It wasn't until Kate walked away with her bag that she realized the salesgirl was judging Kate by her sweater. Foiled by Hello Kitty again. That bright yellow cat with very few facial features was ruining her day.

The lines at the stores throughout the mall were ridiculous. People would stare at their phones, their watches, tap their foot, huff and sigh. There was only one store in the mall that didn't have a long line, Captain Atomic's Comics. Kate wandered in and perused the racks.

Posters in bright, primary colors—deep blues, lush reds, and vibrant yellows—adorned the walls. Almost all of them featured men and women striking powerful poses. There were scantily clad women with swords and broad-shouldered men cutting their way through legions of undead soldiers. Superheroes were lifting trucks over their heads, swinging through the city on webs, or punching their foes.

There were life-size mannequins of Superman, Batman, and the Incredible Hulk. The store was filled with toys and other superhero paraphernalia, bat-shaped boomerangs, web-shooters, and a green bow and arrow set on the wall.

Kate was going to get a gift card for her cousin when she saw him riffling through a long, white box of back issues wrapped in Mylar bags.

"Phil."

He looked up at her and smiled. Phil grabbed her and hugged her. The zipper of his coat snagged on her new scarf, and they were instantly entangled.

"Whoops. I think we're stuck."

Phil tried to break from her embrace, but she moved with him. She tried hard not to tear the delicate threads of the new scarf. It was getting difficult to get unstuck without snagging it.

Phil yanked on the zipper.

Kate exclaimed, "Careful."

They moved together as a unit. Kate wound her finger around his jacket's zipper and carefully untangled the threads. Finally, she broke free. They stood a foot apart.

Phil was fit and trim. He did Jjiu-Jjitsu, yoga, and cross-trained. Every year he flew to San Diego and walked around Comic-Con dressed as Captain America or Spider-Man when he was slimmer. Kate drove down to San Diego to meet him for dinner once, but he showed up in costume. Ever since "the cosplay incident," she would meet him in La Jolla or Laguna Beach where he would show up in street clothes.

One of the things she admired most about her cousin is that several times a year, Phil would don his red, white, and blue costume and entertain the kids at the cancer center. Kate lavished a slew of hearts on his Instagram page every time he posted from the Connecticut Children's Medical Center in Hartford. He made a dashing hero. Outside of his costume, he was a bit on the awkward side. He was more Clark Kent than Superman.

Phil sang, "Happy to be stuck with you."

Kate laughed. It was a hearty, genuine laugh. It was good to see a familiar face—a familiar face she liked.

He queried, "What are you doing here?"

"I'm home for Christmas. I thought you knew."

"Not here, here. Here."

It was evident that he meant Captain Atomic's Comics, not Connecticut.

Kate didn't want to tell him that she was getting him his Christmas gift, because the original present was currently traveling around the world.

She lied, "I was shopping and I saw you as I walked by."

He peered into her shopping bag and saw the slinky new dress.

Phil said, "Aunt Vir called before she got on the boat to tell me that you were going to invite me to the Christmas Ball tomorrow night."

Kate smiled and said, "My mom said that?"

She was stuck. She wanted to see how tonight's date with Herman Schultheiss, DDS went before committing to her cousin.

"Funny story. I lost my front tooth."

Phil joked, "I found it. It's right there."

"Look closer."

After inspecting her mouth, he grimaced.

"Yeesh."

"I knocked out my front tooth. Anyway—"

Before she could continue, Phil joked, "You've got to stop getting into bar fights, missy." He laughed at his own joke and added, "My mom texted me about this. We waited for you last night, but you never showed. Gwen jumped up every five minutes and looked out the window whenever a car went by, like a brand-new puppy. She's worse than Mom with all the worrying. We were all glad you weren't dead in a ditch somewhere."

"Yeah. Thanks for that. Anyway, this is why. My tooth got knocked out of my face last night."

"Too bad it wasn't both of them."

"Phil. That isn't very nice. Just because I missed dinner—"

"No. Because of the song."

"Song?"

He sang a bar of "All I Want for Christmas Is My Two Front Teeth." Then he paused. "I don't know any of the other words of that song except the first line."

Kate smiled. "That's because the song is dreadful."

Phil pointed at her tooth and said, "You're not gonna let a thing like that stop you from going to a party?"

Kate was trying to use it as an excuse. It was going to be her escape clause. However, she quickly realized she had no choice but to ask Phil to accompany her to the biggest social event in all of Bradbury.

"No. It's just that—"

She didn't know how to answer the question without hurting his feelings. Instead, she said, "Hey. We were supposed to have lunch together last time I was in town, and that never happened. Have you eaten?"

"Since you were in town in June? Yes. Many times."

Kate punched him gently on his thick forearm. She said, "I meant today, goofball."

"Actually, I'm on my lunch hour now. I couldn't get here on Wednesday, so I had to come today." He glanced at the time on his phone and added, "I've only got another twenty minutes."

"Food court?"

"Sure." He added, "When do you want me to pick you up tomorrow night?"

She sighed and said, "Seven."

"Cool."

Phil picked up a comic wrapped in a protective sleeve. He was overjoyed. "Avengers issue sixty-two. First appearance of the Man-Ape. It's not in mint condition, but it's decent. And, hey, it's only a buck. I gotta get this."

Phil headed to the register. Kate sighed and said under her breath, "I'm happy to be stuck with you."

Hard Knocks

Before heading back to the house, Tony decided to get a quick workout at the gym. He located the closest LA Fitness on his phone. The gym sat on the periphery of the North Coast Mall, ironically situated next to a Cheesecake Factory. Parking at the mall was awful, but he didn't mind walking across the lot to the building, even though it was a brisk seven degrees.

Once he got inside, he noticed the place was relatively empty. The parking lot was full, but they were mostly mall shoppers commandeering the gym's parking spaces. This late in December, most people had given up their workout routines in favor of office parties and other social gatherings. Buffalo chicken dip and Betsy Ann chocolates trumped burpees and butterfly curls. They'd all be back—in force—at the beginning of the New Year, crowding out the gym's most faithful members.

Tony rode a stationary bike next to a bank of giant windows. While it was very cold outside, the sun was shining and the rays felt warm on his face. He pedaled for an hour. During the cool-down, he watched a beautiful woman, hunkered down with shopping bags, walking across the parking lot, talking on her cell phone.

He wasn't sure if it was the dark hair or the turquoise scarf that he noticed first, but he recognized her. It was the woman he knew only as the Cookie Tray Girl. He jumped off the bike and rapped against the window.

She kept walking. He knocked louder. The glass vibrated after each knock, a reverberating wobble. She turned and saw him. She held her phone to her chest. She mimed the word, "Me?"

He smiled and waved. She halfheartedly waved back. When she smiled back at him, he noticed the solid white square in the front of her mouth. Now, he was convinced it was her.

She smiled, continued walking, and resumed her phone conversation. She offered him no sign of recognition. Tony realized she had only seen him when he was dressed as Santa. He threw down his towel and darted through the building.

He bolted to the door in an attempt to catch up with her, but a large group of older women descended on the gym. Seventeen senior women entered at once. They wore matching pink track suits, the jackets emblazoned with the logo "The Silver Splashers"—in silver, naturally. Underneath, in smaller print, it read "Senior Swim Team."

Tony tried to weave through the elderly swimming group. He dodged a woman with a large straw bag carrying towels, wearing a one-piece swimsuit with a pleated skirt, and a bathing cap covered with plastic flowers. He swerved but nearly collided with a short, stout woman who was proportionally shaped like a mailbox. By the time he reached the parking lot, his mystery woman was gone. She'd simply vanished.

Once outside, he was hit by the cold wind that blew hard against his athletic apparel, a loose pair of navy blue shorts and a bright white tee, drenched with sweat. The wet shirt clung to his body as the cold wind ripped through the parking lot. He shivered and headed back inside.

He could not understand how she'd disappeared. One minute she was there and gone the next. He also couldn't understand why he so urgently wanted to get her attention. It started to dawn on him that he would most likely never see her again. The thought frustrated him, angered him.

He went up to second floor of the gym and lifted weights. He desperately tried to work off his sudden and inexplicable bout of anger.

Hide

After a quick bite with Phil and two hours and thirty minutes of rigorous shopping, Kate, satisfied with her purchases, left the mall. Her lunch with Phil made her feel awful about missing her dinner with her aunt and the rest of the family. She realized she should have never left the house without the cell phone. The guilt began to overwhelm her. On the way to the car, she dialed Gwen, secretly hoping her cousin wouldn't pick up. She didn't want to explain the mess her life had become. She'd lost her job, her luggage, and her front tooth. It was suddenly more than she could bear.

"Kate?"

"Gwen. I wanted to—"

"Kate. It is you. We were so worried. My mom called this morning and explained everything."

"Yeah. I just ran into your brother at the mall and…"

Kate trailed off. She heard someone knocking.

"Kate?"

"Hold on a sec. Some weirdo is waving at me."

Kate saw the handsome stranger waving at her from behind the glass window at LA Fitness.

"Sorry about that. This dude really wanted to get my attention, but I think he's mistaken me for someone else. He's a really attractive weirdo, but I don't know him from Adam."

"Fornadum? Is that Latin?"

"What?"

"Fornadum. What is that?"

"I said: From. Adam."

Gwen laughed and added, "Sorry. There's a lot of wind. Where are you?"

"I'm in the pa—uh-oh."

"Now what?"

Kate saw the husky woman returning to her yellow Jeep. She ducked behind a big black Subaru.

Kate whispered, "I'm gonna have to call you back."

Gwen panicked, "Kate? What is it? What's going on?"

"I'll call back in five minutes. I swear."

Kate disconnected the call. She peered around the front bumper and watched the husky woman pack bags into the back of the Jeep. The cold wind continued to blow. She crouched down low and shivered.

Just then, a woman and three children arrived at the Subaru. They looked down at Kate.

She looked up at them and said, "Shhh. I'm playing a really important game of hide n' seek right now."

The family merely stared at her, their eyes wide, their mouths agape.

She would have to call Gwen back, even though her life seemed messier than it did a minute ago.

Ball

Tony, with his gym bag slung over his shoulder, sauntered into the kitchen as Natalie was putting the leash on Riley.

"I'm walking down to the Millers' house to pick up the girls," Natalie said. "Are you hungry?"

Tony nodded. "Starving."

"I was catching up on some laundry while the girls were at their party. I didn't make anything for dinner. How do you feel about pizza?"

"Sure. Whatever."

Pizza felt like the wrong move after ninety minutes at the gym, but he didn't want to be a nuisance. Tony and Natalie grew up in Boston's North End. There was no way pizza in Connecticut was going to match up.

Natalie held out her hand, palm open and said, "Keys?"

He reached down into his pocket to fish the keys out and he found the envelope with the tickets inside. He pulled it out and showed them to Natalie.

"Hey. I have to give you this. It's tickets to some ball."

Riley started jumping up and down. The dog ran in circles, stopped, looked at him, and ran back around in circles.

Natalie sighed. "Now you've done it. You said B-A-L-L in front of him." She carefully spelled out the word "ball" in front of the dog.

Riley stopped, wagged his tongue, and stared at Tony.

"No way. Your dog does not know the word ball."

At the utterance of the sacred word, Riley got frantic once more. He ran around the kitchen, skidded on a floor mat by the sink, and returned to Tony's side, staring into his eyes.

"Ball."

The dog took off again.

Tony started laughing. Natalie walked over to a woven basket with a small batch of dog toys in it. She grabbed a blue baseball. The ball was covered in tiny pock marks, small indentations where the dog had bitten into it.

"I'll get the girls. You are stuck playing fetch in the backyard."

She took Riley off his leash and opened the back door. Riley followed Tony out. It was already dark outside and a few flakes of snow were blowing around.

Tony ran around in the backyard with Riley. A few minutes later, Natalie came outside. She buttoned her coat and shoved her hands in her pockets, watching him play with the dog.

Tony stopped for a minute and said, "Hey. Do you want to go or not?"

Natalie stared at him and said, "I'm leaving now."

Tony threw the ball and Riley bolted after it.

"No. To the thing." He smiled and added, "The thing we shall not name."

"Tony. It's Christmas. There's a million things to do. They have this thing so close to Christmas every year. I've been telling the board to move it, but no one listens. Anyway, someone would have to watch the girls. I'm sure you didn't bring a tux or have a suit of any kind."

Riley bit into the ball and brought it back to Tony, but did not relent. Tony tried to wrestle the ball from the dog's mouth. Natalie continued naming excuses until Tony said, "Could be fun."

"All right. Let me see if Dom's parents are available. They've been wanting to spend more time with the girls anyway."

She turned away to leave and then turned back to him. "Why do you want to go?"

Tony didn't really want to go. He did, however, have an overwhelming desire to "fix" his sister's holiday. He wanted to see her enjoy herself, and the ball might just be the ticket. He stared at her for a second. Then he shrugged and repeated, "Could be fun."

Natalie obviously found his answer acceptable. She shoved her hands in her pockets and strolled toward him.

Tony tried once again to pry the ball from Riley's mouth. The dog's jaws locked on the blue baseball. Tony grabbed the ball and the dog came with it, lifting both ball and dog off the ground.

"I don't think he understands this game," Tony said with a grin.

Date and Nuts

Kate strolled through Castelluccio's Italian Restaurant, feeling confident in her new dress. It was the first time she could remember losing weight at the holidays. Since the day she arrived, she had been running around and not had much time to eat. After the accident, she had been afraid to bite into anything with the temporary crown in her mouth. Tonight, she would enjoy her dinner, even if she ordered something soft. If anything happened to the tooth, she would be with an expert.

Dr. Herman Schultheiss was sitting at the table scrolling through his iPhone. He put the device away, stood up, and pulled out her chair when he saw her.

Kate sat down and smoothed out the linen tablecloth in front of her. Dr. Schultheiss smiled at her and sat back down. She grabbed the large menu and held it in her hand, without opening it.

"Hello, Dr. Schultheiss."

"Please, call me Herman."

Kate pondered it for a moment. It made her think of Herman Munster, the Frankenstein father of the sixties sitcom. She couldn't think of her date as anything but Herman Schultheiss DDS, or, at the very least, Dr. Schultheiss. She would *not* be calling him Herman. *Good lord, what if I marry this dude?* she thought. *What in the hell will I call him?*

Over the PA system, Italian versions of Christmas songs played. The music made her smile.

She gestured with the menu in her hand and said, "My parents used to take us here when we were kids. I haven't been inside this joint in ages. It doesn't look like anything's changed." Kate looked around the dimly lit restaurant. Everything was exactly how she remembered it. "The exposed red brick, candlelight, and big glass jars with all sorts of pickled vegetables around. Boy, I don't know what it is, but Italians love to put food in big glass jars. It's decorative and convenient."

Dr. Schultheiss smiled and said, "It's one of my favorite restaurants in town. They have a tiramisu that is to die for."

Dean Martin's version of "Rudolph the Red-Nosed Reindeer" began to play.

Kate laughed, "This is our song."

Schultheiss grimaced. "What?"

"Rudolph."

Schultheiss stared at her. "I don't understand."

"Rudolph the Red-Nosed Reindeer. This song reminds me of when I walked into your office."

"We weren't playing Christmas music at the office."

"No. Not the song. The TV show. Rudolph. You know. Hermie the dentist?"

Schultheiss was still puzzled. Kate was aghast.

"Have you never seen the Rankin/Bass Rudolph? It's on TV like every year."

"I've never seen it, but I know there's a gay kid who wants to be a dentist on it. I used to be teased about it."

"He's not gay. He's an elf," Kate said. She considered it for a brief moment and added, "Though he's probably gay."

"There was a fellow student at dental school who brought it up every year. I hated that
guy."

Kate replied, "I can't believe you've never seen it."

"When we were younger, my parents took us to Dusseldorf every Christmas. I didn't see many of the famous American Christmas shows and movies. I've only recently seen *It's a Wonderful Life*."

Kate frowned, "I'm not a fan. I don't like that Mr. Potter gets away with it."

Dr. Schultheiss explained, "But Jimmy Stewart's character—"

Kate interrupted, "George Bailey."

"He gets everyone in town to pull money together. It's very sweet."

"But Potter has the old money and the new money. It's a double win for the bad guy. And Uncle Billy's a dipshit."

Schultheiss stared at her. "You have very strong opinions about this movie."

Dean Martin continued to croon. Kate squirmed. "About everything. This song, for instance. Ugh. Why does Santa have a German accent? He sounds like a bad guy on *Hogan's Heroes*."

"So, you don't like the sound of the German language?"

Kate blushed. She tried to repair the damage and added, "No. Um. No. I don't like an Italian singer sticking German words in Santa's mouth."

Dr. Schultheiss stated emphatically, "Santa Claus is German."

Kate tried to backpedal. "I'm simply not a big fan of this song. And this part—Dean-o sounds like he's making up as the words he goes along. It's so frustrating."

"*Sinterklaas*. It is a German word."

Kate realized she really stepped in it.

"It's the whole Rudolph song bugs me. In the show I was telling you about—Santa is

kind of a bully. He's not nice until he needs Rudolph to guide the sleigh with his mutant power—the aforementioned shiny red nose. I mean, seriously, Santa's sleigh didn't have headlights? Don't even get me started on this world-encompassing fog. It couldn't have been foggy all over the world. That's like some supervillain-level shit right there."

"I see. You have very strong opinions about…everything."

Kate leaned back in her chair and said, "That's comedy in a nutshell. Passionate opinions about minutiae. Observing the world in a unique way and making fun of it."

He said, "You seem annoyed by everything."

Kate bolted forward. She tightened. "No. It's completely the opposite. I write down all this stuff and it goes away. You know, when you have to buy stuff at the store and it runs through your head over and over again? 'I have to get eggs, milk, bread. I have to get eggs, milk, bread.' Once you write it down it instantly goes away. It frees your brain up for other thoughts, because you have a written list. That's what comedy is like. It's very meditational."

She didn't want to mention she lost her job as a comedy writer only the other day. Kate bit into a breadstick from the side of her mouth as to not disturb the tooth she referred to as "the chicklet."

The dentist said, "Not everything is a joke."

It stung a little, and she asked, "Are you implying I'm always on?"

Kate knew some comedians who were always "on." They were annoying. They were usually the least funny members of the pack. She realized the dentist was, most likely, unaware of the level of insult he had hurled at her, but it stung nonetheless.

Schultheiss retorted, "Sometimes you have to be serious."

"I can be serious," Kate said. "This is me—being serious."

She twirled her breadstick around for emphasis. The dentist frowned.

Her mouth became a single straight line. She was infuriated. It dawned on her that Herman Schultheiss was a big, fat jerk. She decided she didn't have to spend time with him. There were plenty of old friends and relatives who were fighting for her free time. It was Christmas after all.

She picked her purse up from the floor as he said, "I have a surprise for you." He added, "I got your crown back from the lab. They've gotten their Three D printer back up and running. I can reapply it tomorrow if you're not too busy. I don't have a lot of patients scheduled, so if you come in early, I can get it done and you'll have it for Christmas."

Just then, he noticed that she was collecting her things. He stared blankly at her, but she quickly shot back with, "I was only going to reapply my makeup."

He said, "I wasn't aware you were wearing any."

She smiled and said, "Be right back."

***

In the ladies' room, Kate worked on gathering her wits. She wanted to crawl out the window, but knew she had to be nice. She wanted that tooth. She stared at "the chicklet" in the mirror. Tomorrow night she was going to the fanciest event in town, the Christmas Ball. She didn't want to show up with the big, white, square tooth in her mouth. It didn't curve to the shape of her other teeth. It was a foreign object, and it would look terrible in pictures. She had to have a normal-looking mouth.

She realized she had to behave for the sake of "number nine, the central incisor." She splashed cold water on her face, looked directly into the mirror, and let out a primal scream. It caused a woman in the stall to drop her cell phone into the toilet. Kate heard a splash and a string of expletives. She exited the restroom as quickly as she could.

When she came back to the table, she was as cordial and polite as she could be.

They ordered. She avoided getting anything too expensive. She wanted to be on her best behavior. She kept thinking, *Don't rock the boat. Stay calm, for number nine.*

"So are you enjoying your visit?" he asked.

Kate lied, "Yes. It's been great."

They entered a safe zone about the weather, local landmarks, and visiting with relatives. The server delivered two dinner salads, arugula with goat cheese and candied walnuts. That's when it happened. The loudspeaker blared "Dominic the Italian Christmas Donkey."

Kate grimaced. The doctor smiled. He said, "Go on. I'm sure you want to pick apart this delightful little Christmas song."

She couldn't help herself. She was like Roger Rabbit when he heard "Shave and a haircut." She had to say, "Two bits."

"This song. It's the worst. I don't know how Lou Monte even sold this thing. I can picture him in the recording studio with the producer saying, 'That's it, Lou. Bray louder in the next take, Eee Aww. Eee Aww.' and really try to annoy me with the La, La, La's.'"

A husband and wife at the next table overheard their conversation. They started to giggle. Suddenly Kate had an audience. It's all any true performer ever needs.

"Why is this song so popular? I'm half Italian, and most Italians are quite proud of this little ditty. My ears must be from another country, because I don't get it."

The husband at the next table said, "You tell 'em. I've been telling you this, Hannah."

The woman, Hannah, spoke directly to Herman Schultheiss, DDS, and said, "Don't listen to them. Mark hates the 'The Little Drummer Boy.' Now, honestly, who could hate 'The Little Drummer Boy?'"

Kate sheepishly raised her hand. She said, "I do. Who brings drums to meet a sleeping baby? Besides, why won't anyone leave Mary alone? She just had a baby, for heaven's sake, literally and figuratively. For *heaven's* sake. You got animals, three Magi, and some kid with a drum set. No thanks. I'd want an epidural."

Mark started laughing. Hannah shook her head and laughed. She said, "We have two kids and now that you mention it—"

Dr. Schultheiss was upset. He whispered, "You're making a scene. Can you not be so—"

The entrees arrived. Her gnocchi and his veal parmigiana.

She turned to Mark and Hannah and said, "Gotta go, folks. The main course has arrived."

Hannah turned to her and said, "Ohh. I love their gnocchi."

Mark said, "I've never had it."

Kate grinned. "Don't gnocchi it 'til you've tried it." She turned back to Dr. Schultheiss and said, "Oh my God. You're right. I have a problem."

Pizza Party

Tony was tipping the pizza delivery boy when Natalie and the girls strolled up the sidewalk. Marie shouted, "Pizza."

She ran for the door, swooshing in her puffy down coat.

Tony was cradling four pizza boxes against his chest while trying to stick his wallet back in his pocket with one hand.

The delivery boy smiled, waved, and ran back to his car, passing Natalie and Danielle.

Marie unzipped her coat and let it drop on the floor. Natalie sighed, picked it up, and slung it on the sofa.

Natalie commanded, "Boots."

Marie ran back to the foyer to take off her boots. Danielle was sitting lotus style pulling off her own boots as Riley circled them, investigating the outdoor odors they carried in with them.

Natalie looked at the stack of pizza as she took off her knit cap. "Geez. How many did you buy?"

"I wasn't sure what kinds the kids like."

"You could have texted me."

Tony smiled and said, "This is the part where you say, 'Thanks for dinner, bro.'"

"I don't say 'bro.'"

Tony shook his head and said, "Or 'thank you,' apparently."

She took off one of her gloves and swatted him in the arm with it.

Tony ignored her. "I got one plain, one with pepperoni, one white one with spinach and feta, and one garden veggie."

"You remembered I like white pizza?"

"I don't think that's really pizza. But yeah. This spinach one is for you."

Tony placed the pizzas on the dining room table. He looked down on his white Boston Red Sox jersey and noticed a large splotch of tomato sauce on it.

"Aw man. Dinner is literally *on* me."

The girls laughed as they ran to the table. Riley followed in hot pursuit, barking at their swift movement away from him.

Tony pulled the shirt up to his mouth and tried to suck the sauce from it.

Danielle squirmed and said, "Ew."

He looked up at them and said, "Not bad. I mean it's not like that place on Hanover. You remember the one?"

"Ernesto's?"

"No. That was on Salem. What am I thinking of?"

"Wait," Danielle said. "That's Boston. I remember Grandpa took us there."

Natalie turned to her and asked, "What was the name of the place?"

Danielle shrugged. "I don't know, I was young. I was—like—eight."

Marie yelled, "I'm eight."

Danielle turned to her and said, "See what I mean?"

Tony said, "The defense rests."

"Marie," Natalie asked, "do you remember going to Boston with Grandma and Grandpa?"

The little girl squirmed in her seat, pouted, and then announced, "I'm hungry."

Tony lifted the lid of one of the boxes. Tendrils of steam wafted upward.

"What kind do you like?" he asked.

Marie announced, "Ham and pineapple."

Tony looked at a copy of the menu taped to the lid of the box. He said, "Ham and pineapple. That sounds disgusting. And I ate camel once."

Natalie stared at him. It was the look she gave him whenever he launched into one of his military adventures in front of the girls.

Marie harrumphed and crossed her arms.

Tony sputtered. "I didn't get that kind."

There was a long moment of silence. Danielle and Marie looked at Natalie. She touched Tony on the shoulder and whispered, "It was their dad's favorite."

Natalie cast her eyes downward. She reached for the silver cross she wore around her neck and held it tight.

Tony lifted the lids of each pizza box, presenting each choice to the little girl. Marie crinkled her nose and turned away from him.

Danielle turned to Tony and said, "I'm with you, Uncle Tony, I think fruit on pizza is gross."

Marie yelled, "No," digging into her defiant posture. She avoided Tony's eyes and her arms remained crossed.

Tony sighed, turned to Natalie and said, "This is the part where you say, 'I told you so.'"

Natalie softly said, "I'm not gonna do that."

Tony brightened and said, "Really?"

Natalie winked.

"No. Cos you remembered my favorite."

Natalie grabbed a slice of white pizza and slapped it on to a paper plate and said, "Marie, pick a slice or go to your room."

Marie sulked for a few more seconds. Then, she reluctantly pointed at the plain pizza.

Natalie put a slice on a paper plate and handed it to her youngest daughter.

"Kids," Danielle exclaimed dramatically.

Natalie and Tony turned to her and started laughing.

After Dinner Mint

Kate was overjoyed when dinner ended. The check came and she insisted on paying for it. She didn't want to be in the doctor's debt, not more than she already was.

He relented far easier than she thought he should have. Kate handed the server her credit card. As the server walked away with the card, she felt a twinge of guilt. She had been spending a lot this weekend and remembered she no longer had a job.

Earlier that day, on her way back from the mall, after she'd called Gwen back and assured her she was okay, she talked to the show's producers on the phone. The network was going to run the three remaining unaired episodes of *The Matt Zimmerman Show* and she would be paid until then, but after that, she didn't know where her next paycheck would come from. She should have let Dr. Schultheiss pay for the meal.

They walked outside together. Kate handed her ticket to the valet, who scurried off to collect her car. She buttoned up her jacket as a cold, wintry wind blew.

"So…" Schultheiss said.

She realized he was expecting more from their date. She didn't want to offend him. He was putting her tooth in tomorrow morning, she merely had to play nice for a little bit longer, but she wasn't willing to spend much more time with him.

He stared at her for a long moment. She smiled back at him but kept hoping the kid with her car would show up.

Schultheiss said, "I was hoping we could go back to your place."

Kate tried very hard not to look disgusted. She offered him a gentle, polite smile.

She said, "I'm kinda staying in my brother's room."

Even though it was true, it sounded like a lie. She wanted to kick herself for not being more direct, but she wanted that tooth.

He zipped up his jacket and said, "We can't go to my place. My wife is there."

Kate's mouth fell open.

Schultheiss corrected, "We're separated, but we still live together."

She had an out. She had to think quickly and not offend him.

"I didn't know that. You didn't mention her." After a brief pause she added, "Doctor—I mean, Herman, I'm not looking for anything complicated."

It was still weird calling him by his first name.

He smiled and said, "Neither am I. That's why I like to meet up with out-of-towners."

Kate's cheeks reddened. She said, "I'm not really—I mean I'm originally from here, so I don't think I count."

He rolled his eyes. "Oh, come on. You're from L.A. You're in show business. You're supposed to be—you know—easy."

She scolded, "Doctor Schultheiss."

She wanted to kick him in the groin, slap his face, or punch him in the stomach. Maybe all three. But she thought about her tooth. Her *damn tooth*.

He almost apologized. "I didn't mean it the way it came out. My situation is complicated. Caroline and I aren't sleeping together."

Kate nearly had to hold her chin up to keep her mouth from dropping open. She tried to be sympathetic and said, "I'm sure that must be hard for you."

She didn't want to be consoling but couldn't help herself. It was an awkward and tense moment. She let him move in closer. She assumed they were going to hug it out, but instead, he grabbed her and pulled her close right as the valet pulled up with her car. He kissed her hard, and, against her better judgment, she relented and let him. It had been a while since someone had kissed her. She didn't want it to be like this. Kate didn't know what to do. Slapping him seemed off-limits, but letting him continue seemed worse.

Then, the dentist jammed his tongue into her mouth. Her eyes widened. That's when she felt the temporary tooth wiggle. It wiggled again.

Kate exclaimed, "Hey."

Dr. Schultheiss pulled back. He winced and realized that he had something in his mouth. He spit the temporary tooth out into his hands.

He handed it to her. A string of saliva connected his hand to hers.

He said apologetically, "My bad."

She refused to take the saliva-covered tooth into her hands.

"I might have some temporary epoxy in my car if you want to repair it for the evening."

Kate joked, "I bet you say that to all the girls—the toothless ones, at least."

Dr. Schultheiss smiled. "Walgreens has something that would work. I could write down the name of it."

Kate shook her head and said, "I'm just going to go to bed." She turned back to him and added, "Alone."

Dr. Schultheiss shoved his hands in his pockets and turned away from her.

"You have my number if you change your mind."

He stared at her, awaiting a change of heart. She wanted to say, "I won't. Thanks," but decided against it.

The valet, a young high school girl, pulled Kate's rented Kia up to the curb. She came to a sudden stop in front of them.

Kate said, "This is me."

Once again, she lisped the word "sorry." Even though she was angry and not sorry at all.

Kate handed a few bucks to the valet, got in the car and sped away.

Get it at Gimbels

Tony tiptoed down the stairs. It was two in the morning, and his sleep pattern was still disrupted from his international travel. When he got downstairs, he heard noises in the living room and saw the blue glow of the television. Natalie was awake, wrapping presents and watching a group of teenagers talking by a row of lockers.

Tony heard a skittering across the wooden floor. He turned to see the little black dog had followed him down the stairs.

Tony sat down next to Natalie and didn't say a word. He watched the television for a few moments.

Riley sat beneath him for a short time. Then, the dog jumped up on the sofa and sat in the small crevice between them. He circled around the small space and plopped down with a large sigh.

Tony stroked the dog's soft fur and gave him a good scratch around his collar. The dog's eyes rolled back in his head. Tony looked over at Natalie.

She glanced over at him and said, "Shut up."

He smiled and responded, "I didn't say anything."

He pushed his shoulder into hers. She nudged back and then unfurled a large swath of bright red wrapping paper on the coffee table, grabbed the scissors, and started cutting it into smaller sections.

"I have to use a different wrapping paper on the girl's presents, because last year Marie said, 'Santa uses the same wrapping paper you do, Mommy.'"

"What did you say?"

"I said there was a sale at Gimbels."

"*Gimbels?*"

Natalie laughed and then said, "I panicked, okay? *Miracle on Thirty-Fourth Street* was on the night before."

"So now when they find out there's no Santa Claus, they'll also learn that there hasn't been a Gimbels in—what—a hundred years?"

"Fifty maybe. I don't know. Google it. Besides, I've lived in Bradbury too long. I wasn't going to tell them I got the Christmas paper at the Dollar Store."

Tony smiled. "There's still some Filene's bargain basement left in the old girl? You haven't gone completely native."

"I don't know. The other day, I let the gas station attendant pump my gas."

"They still do that here?" he asked with feigned horror.

"Yes. They still do that."

"Are you sure you didn't let some homeless dude fill up your tank?"

Natalie shook her head and resumed wrapping presents. She taped up the corners of a shirt box. Tony gazed at the screen.

Natalie retorted, "The girls. They're clever." She thought for a moment and added, "And now they outnumber me."

Tony took it all in. He went back to watching television. He inquired, "What is this?"

"You know it's my go-to show when I'm sad. Bunch of teenagers with superpowers."

Tony wrapped his arm around his sister and they sat in silence for a long while. Riley crawled into Tony's lap and nodded off.

Natalie looked down at the dog and said, "Traitor."

Egg on Her Face

Kate had very few Christmas rituals, but every year during the holidays, Kate and Drew would usually go to Mac's Diner for breakfast. Traditionally, it was on the first day they were both back in town together. Depending on their work schedules, one would invariably arrive a day or two before the other.

This morning, Kate was missing her brother more than usual and decided to do their traditional brother/sister brunch, sans brother.

Mac's was the kind of diner you'd find right off the Jersey Turnpike. It was formerly owned and operated by Nikos Mnesiphilos (AKA Mac), a large Greek man with a raging temper. His daughter, Artemisia, took over two years ago. There had been much less yelling and screaming coming from the kitchen ever since. Mac's had the best breakfasts in town. Kate always ordered the Greek omelette, with spinach, onion, tomato, and feta. It came with a heaping mound of hash browns and a thick slab of toasted Italian bread.

Without Drew, breakfast, while hearty and delicious, was a melancholy affair. She kept thinking of some of their private jokes, and the way they would imitate Nikos swearing in Greek. Since neither of them knew the language, they would gesture and spout off gibberish while looking angry. Drew was, without a doubt, her best audience. He would chuckle and snort. Every year, he would laugh so hard, milk or orange juice would squirt out of his nose. It was always her crowning achievement of each of their annual breakfasts.

This year, it was quiet at her table.

Kate reluctantly ordered her usual, even though she knew it was going to be difficult to eat without her central incisor. She picked up the silver napkin holder and stared at her unusual smile in its reflection. It was only one tooth, but the hole felt cavernous in her mouth.

She was so angry at Dr. Herman Schultheiss.

The bell above the door jingled as new patrons entered the diner. She looked up and saw Mr. and Mrs. Beckett, her mom's neighbors. Kate grew up living next to the Becketts. Years ago, she was their son Timothy's babysitter.

Kate hunkered down in the booth, with the menu up to her face, in a last-ditch effort to avoid them. It was too late.

Roberta "Bobbie" Beckett was a perky, plump woman. Though she was almost always smiling, her grin widened when she noticed Kate in her usual booth.

Bobbie announced, "George. Look. Look who it is. It's little Kate Nolan."

Bobbie's husband George removed his glasses and smiled at Kate.

He exclaimed, "It is. I'll be. I almost didn't recognize her without her usual sidekick."

George Beckett was a tall silver-haired man who wore bright, short-sleeved golf shirts, no matter how cold it was outside.

Bobbie turned to her husband and said, "Andrew took Virginia on that mother/son cruise. That sounds so wonderful. I'm so envious."

Bobbie turned back to Kate and said, "The only place Timmy and I go together is church." She nudged her husband. "When this one is out golfing or playing tennis at the club."

George joked, "Here she goes."

George waved at another couple in the diner and wandered over to them while Bobbie continued to talk at Kate. "Timmy is going to be so mad he slept in this morning."

Bobbie rambled on about Tim and his accomplishments. Her son was going to college now (Georgetown University for pre-law), but he was in town for the holiday break. Bobbie spoke about his grade point average, his extracurricular activities, and his girlfriend. While she continued to smile at Bobbie, Kate felt old, knowing the kid she babysat was in college now. As Bobbie droned on about Tim's girlfriend, she felt profoundly alone.

Kate thought to herself, *Great. Even pimple face is dating.*

Finally, Bobbie said, "And how are you, dear?"

Kate held the menu up to her face and said, "Thingths are good."

Bobbie moved in closer. She said, "What was that?"

Kate placed her hand up to her mouth and said, "I'm terriffffffic."

The server slapped down Kate's plate and dashed off.

Bobbie said, "Oh. Your breakfast is here. I should let you go."

Her sweetness caught Kate off guard, and she said, "No. It'ths okay," without covering her mouth.

Bobbie's eyes widened. She gasped, "Sweetie. Your tooth."

"I'm theeing the dentith right after breakffffath."

Bobbie said, "Are you seeing George's sister? Dr. Therese Beckett-Burke? She's the best dentist in town."

"In hindthite. I really thould have."

Nothing but the Tooth

With nervous trepidation, Kate marched into the Brightside Medical Building. She stood in the lobby and stared at the elevator, pressed the call button, and hung her head low.

A woman with a small boy got on the elevator at the same time. The mother tried to stop him, but the child pressed all the buttons with gleeful determination.

The woman apologized to Kate, but Kate turned to the woman and said, with her lisp, "No big. I'm not in any hurry."

She got off the elevator, zipped into the ladies' room, and brushed her teeth one final time before entering the office. She stared at the gap in her mouth for a long moment before grabbing the last paper towel in the dispenser and wiping the corners of her mouth.

When she finally did arrive, she met with the snarky receptionist, who said, "Your appointment was for ten."

Kate looked at her watch. She was three minutes late. She realized she would never have to see the receptionist again. She felt a sudden rush of boldness and replied, "Three minutesth?? Doesth that even count? That doesthn't count."

The receptionist looked at her, pursed her lips, and returned her attention to her computer monitor.

Kate did not get to bask in her moment of triumph, because Francine, the dental hygienist, greeted her at the door and said, "We can take you back now."

Francine walked her back to one of the offices. Kate sat down in the dental chair and waited for Dr. Schultheiss.

An eternity passed, though it was only seven minutes, and Schultheiss entered.

"Kate. I'm glad you could make it. Let's pop this sucker in."

He held a soft, blue cloth that held the crown inside like a jewel.

Dr. Schultheiss did most of the talking. Kate nodded as he explained how the crown was carved into the shape of her original tooth. He talked about how newer technologies have sped the process up since he graduated medical school. He talked about lasers and 3D printers and all sorts of techno-babble.

He did not mention last night. For a moment, she felt safe. He was acting like a professional dentist and not the jerk she was out with last night.

Then, while his hands were in her mouth, he said, "I'd like to see you again while you're still in town."

Her reply sounded a lot like Rocky Balboa after a fight, but it was clear enough for Schultheiss. He heard her say, "Uh. Okay."

She wanted to kick herself.

In an open-mouthed, guttural speech, she managed to say something that meant, "I'm in town 'til New Year's Eve. We should hang out."

If she were upright, she *would have* kicked herself.

Schultheiss admitted, "I will be hanging with Caroline for Christmas, but afterward, we should meet up for a drink."

Kate gave him the thumbs-up. She deserved a third swift kick in the ass.

Buttered Up

Tony pushed a shopping cart around the grocery store. The cart had one squeaky wheel that wobbled when he rounded the corners. The store was packed. He had never seen so many people in one small space before. It was tight trying to maneuver the cart around the throngs of shoppers.

Tony stood over a bin full of frozen turkeys. He stared at them. He didn't know if there was a surefire method of picking the perfect turkey. He moved a few around and selected one he thought was the right size. The package claimed it was fifteen pounds but was probably heavier since it was frozen solid. An older woman rolled her cart over to the bin. She tried to lift one with one hand, but Tony stopped her.

Tony said, "Ma'am, would you like me to put one in your cart?"

"I'm sorry. If you don't mind. I did something to this arm." With her good hand, she pointed at the other arm that dangled by her side.

"Not at all," Tony said with a smile. He hoisted a turkey up and added, "How about this one?"

She nodded and said, "Yes. That's perfect."

"There's just one problem. How are we going to get it out of your cart?"

"My niece is with me. She's in oil."

Tony joked, "Exxon? Sunoco?"

"I mean… she's picking out a nice olive oil. You know they have so many flavors now. It used to be one kind of oil and one kind of vinegar. Now there's like seven hundred different kinds of each. I have a bottle of Sorrento Lemon Olive Oil and a bottle of blueberry-infused balsamic vinegar now. You can't use them together, though. They make your salad too fruity."

Tony smiled at her. "I'm glad you have someone to help you bring the turkey into your house. Have a nice holiday, ma'am." Tony waved good-bye and maneuvered his shopping cart down the aisle to the next item on the list Natalie had written for him.

Tony held a can of pumpkin pie filling in his hands while Perry Como sang, "There's no place like home for the holidays" on the store's PA system.

He heard a woman in the next aisle say, "Like this. This is a perfect example. He says the traffic is terrific. Who says that about traffic? Wow. We're going to be stuck on the turnpike for hours. Gee, the traffic is terrific."

He covered his mouth, trying not to laugh.

The woman continued, "I'm telling you, Aunt Vi, we need some new Christmas songs."

Her gripe about the Perry Como song tickled him. She sounded vaguely familiar, but he assumed it was a coincidence.

After he secured every item on the list, Tony swerved his shopping cart into a long line at checkout. He scanned the local magazines on the rack and thumbed through a *TV Guide* while he waited.

When it was his turn, he hauled the fifteen-pound frozen turkey onto the conveyor belt and proceeded to unload the contents of the cart with one hand, and hold the *TV Guide* in the other.

The cashier pointed at the small, glossy magazine and said, "Do you want that, too?"

He shook his head but held on to the *TV Guide*. "I haven't really watched TV in some time. I don't really miss it."

The cashier looked at him as if he were speaking a foreign language. The perky young girl inquired, "What do you do in your spare time?"

"I keep busy."

He did not feel like telling the eighteen-year-old cashier he had returned from a warzone not even a week ago, and could not name one housewife from any of the trillion reality shows, nor did he know which celebrities were doing the cha-cha on *Dancing with the Stars*.

He returned the magazine to the rack. He couldn't imagine a situation where he would want to buy a magazine about television.

A few minutes later, he was packing all the groceries into the trunk of Natalie's car when he got a text from her that read: "Need more butter. LOL if they have it."

LOL? It took him a few minutes to realize she meant Land O' Lake's butter and that she wasn't 'Laughing Out Loud' about it.

He thought long and hard about ignoring her text. He could pretend he didn't see it and drive back to her house, but then he'd have to probably go back out again for it. He thought about it for another moment. Then he let out a loud sigh, snapped the trunk shut, and went back into the grocery store.

Extra Virginal

After her dental appointment, Kate drove over to her aunt's house. She got there right as Violet was backing out of the driveway.

Kate parked on the street and ran over to her car. Violet rolled down the window and said, "Kate. Nice to see you. I'm on the way to the store to pick up a few things for our Christmas dinner."

"Do you want me to come with?"

"I don't want you to spend your Christmas vacation in the grocery store. You should do something fun."

"Open up. I'm coming."

"If you're sure you don't mind."

"Open."

Kate got in the passenger seat and buckled up.

"It will certainly be easier with you along," Violet said. "I pulled a muscle getting a box of Christmas decorations out of the attic. It must have only weighed thirty pounds. It's a bitch getting old. Let me tell you. My left arm is completely useless."

Kate smiled and said, "Um. Maybe I should drive?"

"Oh. Your tooth is normal again."

***

In the store, Kate expounded on the details of her bad date. "I admit I was nervous and maybe said some stuff I shouldn't have said. I kinda went into a tirade about Christmas music."

"A whole tirade? I don't think I understand."

"Well, it's complicated."

They stopped in canned goods. Violet said, "I hate to ask, but could you reach the olives?" The olives were on the top shelf. Violet said, "I've got Kalamata and Spanish olives from the olive bar, but we need a can of those ridiculous black ones that don't taste like anything."

"These?" Kate grabbed the canned black olives and added, "Yes. You have to have them. Drew and I used to put them on our fingers and pretend to be wicked witches. Looking back, I should not have been so shocked when he came out to me."

"It's the only kind Dax will eat."

Violet looked down at the cart and asked, "Did we pass the extra-virgin olive oil?"

Kate said, "I'll run back for it."

"The darker the yellow, the better. Matter of fact, if they have a slightly green one, get it."

"Um. Okay."

Violet said, in complete and utter seriousness, "Meet me by the crescent rolls."

***

Kate ran down and perused the oils. There was a dark green one. She turned to a tall woman in a red coat and asked, "Pardon me, do you know if this is a good kind?"

The woman said, "Why yes. That's the kind I buy."

"Green is better than yellow?"

"Yes. This one is cold pressed."

Kate shrugged and confessed, "I didn't know there was so much to it."

She grabbed the fancy one from the high shelf, turned back to the woman, and said, "Thanks."

Kate rejoined Violet in the bread aisle. Violet whispered, "I met a very attractive man by the turkey bin."

"Go Vi."

"Not for me. For you."

"After last night, I am swearing off men for a while."

"This one was even better looking than—" Violet whispered, "Doctor Schultheiss."

"He's not Voldemort. You can say his name."

"This one had muscles."

"Violet. I had no idea you were such a horn dog."

The PA system blasted Perry Como's "(There's no place like) Home for the Holidays."

Kate sighed.

Tangles

Tony sat in the corner of the room with a tangled mass of Christmas lights on his lap. One half of the strand was lit, the other was not. He kept plugging lights into the tester to see which one would get the whole jumbled pile blinking in unison.

Natalie hunched over a large plastic bin, picking through boxes of ornaments. The girls stood at her side. Riley placed his two paws up on the side of the bin and peered in. When the dog realized the box did not contain food of any sort, he lost interest and went in search of a partially gnawed chew toy under the sofa.

Marie grabbed the Little Mermaid ornament and placed it on the tree.

Danielle shouted, "No. The lights go on first." Danielle removed the ornament from the tree.

Marie yelled, "Mom."

Natalie sighed. "Sweetie, you have to wait 'til your uncle Tony can untangle the lights."

Tony grumbled, "More *if* than *when*."

Marie grabbed the ornament back from Danielle. Marie stamped her foot. "It's my favorite. The fish girl. I'll just hold her."

"Mermaid, dummy." Danielle barked.

"Let's not do the name-calling thing. Do you want me to get Santa on the phone and tell him to skip our house this year?"

The girls froze in their tracks and looked over at their mother in horror. Tony stifled a laugh. He shot Natalie a look.

"I'll take 'Things Mom Used To Say' for one hundred, Alex."

Natalie would not return his gaze.

The entire strand of lights went dark. Tony plugged a light into the open socket and the whole jumble turned on.

Natalie shook her head. "Yeah. But now you have two blue ones together. Can't you find a red, yellow, or green one for that space?"

"It's gonna have to do."

Then, half the strand remained on while the other half blinked.

Tony was forlorn. He hadn't solved the Christmas light problem. He groaned. "I probably should untangle them first."

Marie pulled another ornament out of the box. She held it tight in her other fist.

"This guy's my favorite."

Danielle commented, "I thought Ariel was your favorite?"

Natalie was clearly resigned.

"Marie is allowed to have more than one favorite, Danielle," Natalie said.

Marie showed the new favorite to Tony. It was Buzz Lightyear.

Tony turned to Natalie and said, "Buzz. Do you remember that Thanksgiving in New York?"

Natalie chuckled and added, "How can I forget?"

Danielle looked at Natalie and then back to Tony.

Tony started, "So I was in high school and your mom was going to Columbia University in New York City—"

Natalie laughed harder.

"Your mom invited me down to the city because her sorority and your dad's fraternity were going to be balloon handlers in the Macy's Day Parade this one Thanksgiving."

Natalie smiled. "I had just started dating your father. Dommy talked me into some crazy stuff back then, including being a balloon handler at the Macy's Day Parade…"

Tony grinned. "As long as I live, I will never forget it. Nearly flying off Fifth Avenue."

Natalie added, "You have to know that your Uncle Tony was not all big and buff like he is now. He was a scrawny thing weighing about one hundred pounds."

Tony nodded and said, "I drink my milk."

"Anyway, the Sigs and the Kappas were put on the—"

Tony interrupted, "Do you want to tell the story?"

"Oh. No. Go 'head."

"We were handling the Buzz Lightyear balloon. Picture that ornament, only—picture him the size of a school bus."

Natalie held up two fingers and chimed in, "More like two school buses."

"There weren't enough of us," Tony said.

"A lot of kids signed up but not all of them showed."

"The balloon was simply too big. One strong gust of wind and a few of us were airborne. I remember this girl—"

Natalie supplied, "Denise."

"Yeah. Denise and I were near the back. And several times our legs would be off the ground. A bunch of us were dragged down two city blocks until the balloon crashed into the side of that building."

"I think it's a CVS now." Natalie was holding her sides. She said, "I remember looking back and seeing both of you bouncing down the street, legs dangling in the air, a group of seasoned professional balloon handlers running after us trying to grab the reins—" Natalie laughed so hard she could no longer contribute to the story. She doubled over and

announced, "I think—I'm going to pee."

Tony covered his mouth trying to contain his own laughter. After a few minutes, Natalie would slow down, then look over at him and start laughing all over again. The girls were silent.

Danielle and Marie stared at them.

After a prolonged silence, Tony said, "I guess you had to be there."

As Natalie riffled through the bin, a giggle or two would burst out as she unfurled a swath of garland.

She said, "Speaking of flying through space—I'm missing my Star Trek ornaments."

"You're such a nerd." Tony shook his head with a smile.

Danielle gasped, "Uncle Tony. That's name-calling."

"Oh, right."

"Can you see if they're up in the attic?"

Tony set aside the jumble of lights and rose. Natalie followed him up the staircase.

Tony stood in the second floor hallway and pulled on a latch. He unfolded the attic ladder and climbed up.

Natalie called out to him. "There should be a red shoebox marked 'Christmas ornaments' up there on the right."

"Is there a light switch?"

"Yes, but to get to it you have to walk on the rafters because the attic is mostly insulation and drywall and probably can't support your—"

CRASH.

Tony fell halfway through the ceiling. From the waist up he was in the attic. His legs, however, dangled above the second-floor hallway. Chunks of debris were strewn below him, a white, powdery dust raining down.

She choked out, "Are you okay?"

Even though he couldn't see her, Tony knew Natalie was trying really hard not to laugh. He could hear little puffs of air escape her lungs as she tried to speak.

The commotion caused the girls and Riley to run up the steps. The dog barked at his legs as they dangled from the second-floor ceiling. More bits of plaster and paint showered down on the hallway.

Natalie posited, "Are you stuck?"

Tony replied, "Not really. I can't seem to grab on to anything to boost myself up. It'd be easier to slip through the hole, but I don't want to make it bigger."

Natalie said, "It's already a pretty big hole. You want me to put some pillows down?"

"No. I got it."

Tony wiggled out of the hole and fell on the floor with another resounding crash.

Natalie asked, still through fits of giggles, "Are you all right?"

He lifted his head up and assessed his body for any damage. He nodded and said, "I'm fine. In Kabul, I had to jump out of a three-story building because of a suicide b—"

Natalie shot him the Look. He zipped it.

The powdery white dust from the paint and drywall continued to sprinkle down on his head, like an indoor snowfall.

"Gravity is no longer your friend."

Don't Knock the Goats

Kate admired herself in the mirror. She was in her new tight black dress from Nordstrom's. She smiled. Her new crown looked perfectly at home in her mouth. Schultheiss was an ass, but he did a good job.

Kate admired the rest of her ensemble. She'd "borrowed" a silver necklace and earrings from her mother's jewelry box. They were exquisite pieces that perfectly accented her black dress. While she was at it, she decided to "borrow" her mother's black velvet wrap. It had a red satiny lining.

The doorbell rang at ten to seven. Phil stood in a black tuxedo, black overcoat, black leather gloves. and a jaunty Greek fisherman's cap.

Kate was astonished when she opened the door. He looked much more dapper than Kate had expected. He must have thought the exact same thing of his cousin because he said, "Wow. You clean up good."

She turned around and most of her back was exposed. She said, "Can you—?"

Phil zipped up the back of her dress.

"What do you girls do when I'm not around?"

"You zip up a lot of women's dresses, cuz?"

"I probably unzip more of them."

"You're such a player."

"I haven't been with a girl since June. I hooked up with a Catwoman at Comic Con."

"How many cats did she have?"

"No. She didn't have cats. She was dressed like the super-villain, Catwoman."

"Oh."

"She had a leather outfit and a whip. I found out later that the whip wasn't just a prop." Phil rubbed his own butt, as if it still hurt months later.

"We're entering TMI territory here. You ready to go?"

Phil opened the door for her. On the way out, he said, "When we get there, I'm going straight to the silent auction table. I heard Joanie at work say that they have some really good items on it this year. Box seats at Dunkin' Donuts Park for the Goats' games, a weekend in Belize, and a six-burner, stainless steel barbecue grill."

"I am going to bid on a spa package. I could really use a hot rock massage."

Phil joked, "Is that real? That sounds like a Fred Flintstone thing."

"Whereas going to a Harvard Yard Goat's game is so cool."

"Don't knock the Goats."

As soon as he said it, he realized he had to follow up in song. He began singing a parody of "Don't rock the boat," except he changed the lyrics to "Don't knock the goats."

"Are you ready, Phil?"

He kept singing as Kate opened the front door. "I'm going to leave without you."

"Why do you hate music?"

Phil marched outside, but he couldn't help himself, he sang, "Don't knock the goats. Don't knock the goats, BAY-BEE."

Sugar Plum Fairies

Tony was at the top of the stairs when he heard Big Dom and Marilyn DeNunzio enter the house.

Marilyn said, "Knock, knock," instead of actually knocking. Big Dom followed her in. He was carrying bags. The girls rushed toward them, screaming, "Nunny and Pap are here. Nunny and Pap are here."

Of course, Riley trailed after them, barking. A few seconds later, Natalie appeared, hugging her now ex-in-laws.

Tony continued down the staircase and greeted them as Natalie said, "You remember my brother Anthony."

Tony extended his hand, but Big Dom gave Tony the stink eye. Tony quickly retracted his hand.

The older man said, "You ought to be ashamed of yourself."

Tony looked down at the navy blue suit he borrowed from the closet and said, "I completely understand. I have a pair of nice jeans I think I could wear instead."

Big Dom ignored him and said, "Marty Kasiewicz is on the town council. He and I went to high school together."

Natalie sensed danger and led Marilyn and the girls into the other room. Riley followed.

Tony insisted, "I don't know a Marty Kaza... What was it?"

"He's been playing Santa in Bradbury for seventeen years. *Seventeen*."

"Oh. That."

Big Dom then noticed the suit. "That's Dominic's. Marilyn. Grab the kids. I can't stay in this house another minute."

Marilyn and Natalie returned to the foyer.

Marilyn insisted, "Just sit down and have some hot cocoa."

Big Dom pointed to the suit. "Do you see this?"

Marilyn looked at Tony standing in Dom's suit. She turned to Tony and said, "Frankly, it looks better on you."

Big Dom was aghast. He shouted, "Marilyn."

Marilyn shot back, "Big Dom, you're being ridiculous. First of all, everyone knows Marty drinks. Too much if you ask me. And second of all, we all know Dominic was your favorite, but as far as I'm concerned, he abandoned his children. His *children*, Dom. It doesn't matter what he and Natalie were going through, he could have figured something out. You know he hasn't even been by to see the girls since September? Do you remember seeing him here at Marie's birthday? No. He missed it. Just like he missed Halloween and Thanksgiving."

Big Dom fell silent.

Marilyn added, "I left a small gift bag in the backseat. It's for Natalie. Can you go get it?" She turned to Natalie and said, "It's only some lotions, bath salts, and fragrance oils from Bath and Body Works. Nothing really."

Big Dom took the keys out of his coat pocket and went back out the door.

Marilyn took Natalie by the arm and marched her back into the living room. She added, "I thought the girls and I could decorate sugar cookies tonight. I brought Christmas cutouts, sprinkles, and four different colors of icing. Afterward, I'm going to read *T'was the Night Before Christmas*. Won't that be fun?"

The girls jumped up and down. Riley barked. Big Dom dropped the gift down on the hall credenza and plopped down on a La-Z-Boy in the living room with a resounding harrumph. He grabbed a clump of newspaper on the coffee table and hid behind it, reading the day's headlines.

Arrival

Tony got out of the car and handed the keys to the valet. Another valet opened the passenger door for his sister. Tony hiked up his pants as he exited the vehicle. Dom's pants were too big for him. Natalie had bunched up the pants at the hips and fastened bobby pins inside to hold them up, but it wasn't working very well. The suit jacket, however, gathered at the sleeves, exposing half of his finely toned forearms. He felt like an organ grinder's monkey.

When they arrived at the entrance to the grand ballroom, a portly gentleman took their tickets and ushered them inside. Tony tugged on the collar. He should have rented a tux, but the event was "black tie preferred," which meant he could get away with wearing a suit. He just wished he had his own suit and not his ex-brother-in-law's ill-fitting one.

Claire and Beryl greeted them. Tony was busy admiring the ornate décor and giant crystal chandeliers while Claire introduced them to their husbands, Ralph and Stewart. Because he wasn't paying attention, Tony wasn't sure which husband belonged to which woman. Ralph grabbed Tony by the shoulder and said, "Son, let me show you to the bar."

Tony marched off with the older gentlemen while his sister got stuck with Claire and Beryl. He turned to catch the dirty look she tossed him.

Place the Name

Kate strolled around the silent auction table, perusing the selection and sipping a glass of Prosecco. She stared at a wicker basket that had a loofah, bath beads, essential oils, and a gift certificate to a local spa. She wrote her name down on the clipboard for the spa treatment package and circled the table. She noticed a very handsome man looking at the coveted auction item. She could tell he was assessing the overall value of the package and she knew she was going to be outbid.

After he wrote his name down on the clipboard, Kate decided to up her bid. She sauntered back to the spa package looking casual and aloof. She noticed his name on the sheet of paper: Tony Rossi. The name did not ring a bell, but it seemed important to memorize it, in case he tried to outbid her in the auction.

Mayor Rae-Anne Broome stood at the podium onstage and, after a lengthy introduction lauding the accomplishments of the evening's host, invited the emcee, Channel Three weatherman Skip Casanova, to the stage. Casanova went to the microphone and tapped it loudly. The microphone on the podium clashed with the microphone on the lapel of his tux and a feedback loop reverberated through the room. The loud discordant noise caused many people to wince or cover their ears.

Casanova said, "Ladies and gentlemen, please take your seats. Dinner will be served shortly."

Kate knew the silent auction was going to close for dinner and turned to get back to her spa package when she slammed into the handsome man.

He said, "We've got to stop meeting like this."

Kate offered him a polite but discreet laugh. She didn't recognize him. Just then, a stream of cater-waiters flooded in from every entrance. Some carried salad bowls filled with crisp greens, such as endive and arugula, and others filled water and wine glasses. Phil stood up at Table 12 and waved Kate to join him.

The handsome man pointed at his front tooth and said, "Nice replacement, by the way."

She reeled back. She couldn't quite grasp how she could not recognize the Adonis before her. His muscles rippled and strained against the tight suit. He smiled and extended his hand.

The handsome stranger turned back to Kate, smiled, and said, "You don't know me at all, do you?"

She smiled and said, "You're Tony Rossi." She cheated. She had read his name off a sheet of paper not a moment ago.

He smiled broadly.

Kate said, "I should get back to my table."

She couldn't understand how she could have forgotten such a good-looking guy. She backed away from him, but she couldn't stop looking at him.

As he walked away, he said, "Save a dance for me. I'd like to get you out on the floor instead of on the ground."

The comment struck her as impertinent, but she found herself giggling like an idiot.

"Um. Yeah. Sure."

He smiled and walked away.

When she arrived at Table 12, Phil pulled out her chair. She turned to him and said, "Do you know who that is?"

Kate nodded to the handsome gentleman who walked to his table. Phil shook his head. She added, "I don't understand. He knew about my front tooth."

"Maybe he was somebody from high school. I remember the first time you lost that in high school. Volleyball?"

Kate corrected, "Dodgeball."

Phil retorted, "Same thing."

"I didn't recognize the name, though."

Kate put down her Prosecco and picked up her water glass. She took a small sip. A cater-waiter gently placed a salad bowl on her plate with remarkable speed and efficiency. Another waiter placed a basket of bread on the table; white linen covered the hot rolls.

Phil reached for the bread. He uncovered the rolls and snatched a hot multigrain roll from the basket with a small pair of silver tongs. He turned to two other guests who were seated next to them.

Phil said, "Speaking of high school, meet Barbara. She's a retired schoolteacher."

Kate was too distracted to meet Barbara. She muttered, "Where could I possibly have met him?"

Phil continued, "This is her husband Martin."

Kate mumbled, "You don't forget a guy like that, I'm just saying."

Phil added, "Martin is on City Council."

"He was the guy at the gym who seemed so eager to wave to me. I didn't recognize him in the suit. Wait. Suit."

Kate was on the cusp of discovery. She hadn't heard a word Phil and Martin were saying.

Martin added, "Please, call me Marty."

Phil continued to fill Kate in. He said, "You won't believe what Marty here does in his spare time. He's—"

Kate blurted out, "Santa Claus."

Phil's jaw dropped. He said, "How did you possibly know?"

Kate turned to him and said, "What?"

Phil said again, "How did you know that Martin dresses up as Santa?"

Kate stared at Phil as if he had two heads and repeated, "What?"

Marty turned to Kate and said, "That's uncanny. Barb has a birthmark shaped like Texas. Tell us where it is and I'll give you five dollars."

Barb swatted at her husband playfully and said, "Ass."

Marty said, "Don't *tell* her. Now the trick's ruined."

Barb scolded her husband, "You're drunk."

Kate looked at them and then looked back at the handsome man.

She said, "The other day I had this—pedestrian collision—with a dude dressed like Santa Claus. He's over at that table."

Marty leaned in. His curiosity piqued. He asked, "Which man?"

She pointed to the handsome gentleman as he sat down at table three.

Speechless

A cater-waiter delivered surf and turf to Tony's table. Natalie turned to him and whispered, "Take my filet mignon and give me your salmon."

Tony ribbed his sister. He said, in a mocking tone, "Please?"

She whimpered. "Please."

Tony stuck his fork into her filet and nabbed it. Then, he slid his salmon onto her plate. Before relinquishing it completely, he snuck a bite. The salmon melted into his mouth. It was rich and buttery with a hint of a balsamic reduction slathered on the bottom of the fish.

"That's delicious."

Natalie chortled. "No taksie-backsies."

Claire cut her salmon in half and offered Tony the larger piece. He smiled and waved her off. The gesture did not sit well with Claire's husband.

Onstage, Skip returned to the microphone. He tapped on it with a loud thump. Then he adjusted it, and once again an irritating screech resounded throughout the room.

"Ladies and gentlemen, I want to present our award for the Volunteer of the Year."

Claire winked at Skip. Natalie grabbed Tony's arm, hard.

Natalie whispered, "Oh my God. I have a really funny feeling."

Tony said, "Maybe it's the salmon."

Skip continued, "Our volunteer of the year logged over one hundred hours and donated large stacks of toys for underprivileged youth in our area, while raising two girls as a single mom, I might add."

That's when it struck Tony. He turned to his sister. She was beaming. Unshed tears sparkled in her eyes.

Tony was hesitant. Maybe there were other women in the community raising two daughters. He didn't want to assume.

Skip added, "Ladies and gentlemen, it is my distinct honor to introduce our Volunteer of the Year, Ms. Natalie Focareta."

Skip cupped the microphone and looked at Natalie. He waved her up to the stage. The audience applauded.

Natalie walked toward him, kissing and hugging everyone along the way. When she arrived onstage, Skip adjusted the microphone to suit her height. By the time she spoke, tears were streaming down her face. They were tears of joy, but the audience didn't know. Her first sentence didn't help. "It's Rossi now. Natalie Rossi. My divorce was finalized this week."

Skip adjusted his bow tie and cracked, "Hey guys, our volunteer of the year is single."

His pronouncement was followed by awkward silence.

Tony yelled, "Speech."

She waved him off but took the microphone anyway.

"I want to thank everyone at the foundation for nominating me. My brother and I"—she pointed to Tony and continued—"had awesome Christmases growing up. I wanted to give every kid in Bradbury the kind of Christmas we had. You know, my name, Natalie, in Italian, refers to the birth of—"

Just then, two police officers walked down the aisle with Marty Kasiewicz. Marty pointed at Tony.

Natalie said, "Jesus Christ," into the microphone.

One of the police officers placed his hand on Tony's shoulder. He looked up at them mid-bite (the filet mignon was as good as the salmon).

"Sir, we'd like to ask you a few questions."

"What? Why?"

The other officer said, "Down at the station."

He tried to object. "I think there's been some kind of mistake—"

The officer simply said, "Sir?"

Tony stood up. Even though he was confused, he complied with their wishes. He knew better than to question their authority, especially in front of a crowd.

From the stage, Natalie asked, over the microphone, "What's happening? Where are you taking him?"

Skip tried to get the microphone back from Natalie, but she wrestled him for it.

"That's my brother. They're arresting my brother. Wait. Why are they arresting my *brother*?"

Tony looked up at her and shrugged.

Natalie shouted, "Bring him back."

Tony managed to watch Natalie running off the stage, stopping for a moment, then pivoting dramatically before rushing back for her award. She caught his eye for a moment before bolting in his and the officers' direction as he followed them out the door.

Stations

Kate's jaw was agape. She watched the police escort the handsome man she now knew as Tony Rossi out of the ballroom. She turned to Phil and Barbara and said, "What the hell is happening?"

Barbara covered her face with the white table napkin. "I can't believe this is happening. Frankly, I'm mortified." She looked up from behind the linen napkin and when she noticed that a lot of eyes were on her, hid back behind her napkin. "They're all staring at me."

Phil said, "Not everyone."

Kate slapped his arm.

"What is going on?"

Barbara said, "Marty had that young man arrested."

Kate blurted, "What? Why?"

"The two of them had a very public disagreement."

Phil's eyes lit up. He was struck by the sudden realization. He pulled his phone out of his

dinner jacket and called up a clip with a few flicks of his finger.

Phil showed Kate the YouTube video. The video stalled as the one Santa (Marty) went flying into the Christmas tree.

After it ended, Kate turned to Barbara and said, "But he didn't do anything. Wait. Which one is which?"

She pointed to the slightly taller Santa in the video, which resumed after buffering.

Barbara said, "I'm married to that one." She again pointed to the screen.

"And…you're absolutely right. The young Santa didn't do anything wrong except get on my husband's bad side. He's an ass. I should have left when Stephanie graduated high school."

Kate stood and said, "We can't just sit here."

Phil looked up from his filet and put his fork down. He asked, "We're gonna leave? I have a few bids in on the silent auction table."

Marty marched back to the table, slapping his hands together, clearly feeling extremely satisfied.

He watched as Phil stood up next to Kate.

Kate turned to Barbara, and said, "You could come with us."

Phil nudged Kate.

Marty sat down. He said, "Now? It's a party."

Barbara stood up.

Marty stared at her.

Barbara said, "That was awful, Martin. Just awful. That young man wasn't the problem and you know it. Your drinking is the problem."

Everyone was staring, including Skip at the dais.

Marty looked around. His cheeks reddened. He whispered, "Sit down, Babs. You're making a scene."

Barbara was indignant. She yelled, "*I'm* making a scene? I'm making a *scene*? You just had Natalie Focareta's brother escorted out by the police."

Marty gulped. He said, "Focareta? Focareta?"

Phil interjected, "I think it's Rossi now."

Kate's eyes darted from Marty to Barbara to Phil.

"As in Dominic Focareta?" Marty asked.

Barbara nodded. "That's the one."

Marty slurred, "Dominic is one of my best constituents. Donors. I mean…friends."

Barbara said, "I hope you're happy."

She turned and marched out. Kate and Phil followed her.

Desk Set

Outside, in the brisk wintry air, Kate, Phil, and Barbara stood in line behind Natalie as she waited for the valet to bring her car around.

Phil turned to her and said, "Um. Congratulations."

She slapped on the side of the award, waiting impatiently for her car. She turned to him and said, "Um. Thanks. I guess."

Phil said, "Bummer about your...date."

"Brother."

Phil responded, "Yeah. That's right. Brother." After a long pause he added, "Cool."

Kate elbowed him in the side.

Natalie turned to Kate and said, "You're the cookie girl."

"Yep."

"I didn't recognize you all dressed up and with a tooth. Dr. Schultheiss does good work."

"Yeah. But don't ever go on a date with him."

"You went on a date with Herman? On purpose? Good lord. He's handsome and all, but...geez. He's kind of a douche."

"You knew? Why did you recommend him?"

"Cos he has late office hours. Wait. I recommended him for your tooth, not for...um... anything else."

Phil laughed, loudly. Kate elbowed him so hard, air escaped from his lungs.

The valet pulled Natalie's car around. Phil gave the attendant his ticket.

Natalie didn't get in the car. She turned to Barbara and said, "I'm so nervous and angry. I don't think I can drive."

"I'll go with you," she said.

Kate chimed, "We'll follow you down to the station."

***

Seventeen minutes later, the two cars pulled into the Bradbury Police Station parking lot. The four of them gathered in the lot and went in together. Natalie pointed to the restroom sign.

Natalie grabbed her stomach and said, "I think I'm going to throw up."

Barbara escorted her to the restroom.

Kate said to their retreating backs, "We'll try to get some answers"

The police station was decorated with garland. There were a few large, plastic cutouts on the wall: a snowman, Santa's face, and an obligatory menorah.

Kate and Phil found the desk sergeant, Alice Campbell, a short African-American woman in uniform. She was pleasant and cheerful.

"Hello," Phil started. "We're looking for a…perp." He turned to Kate and said, "What's his name again?"

Kate squirmed. "I'm not sure. I knew it a minute ago. It's a champagne name."

Sergeant Campbell said, "I'm sorry. What is this about?"

Kate and Phil heard a commotion in the other room. It sounded like laughter. Sergeant Campbell rose and hobbled over to a door behind her and closed it.

The sergeant said, "Christmas party. Sorry about that." She paused and looked at her police blotter. "Who are you here for again?"

"His name is Tony," Kate said. "Anthony. He was just arrested."

Sergeant Campbell looked at some papers on her desk. "Last name?"

Kate said, "I want to say Rossi? Was it Rossi?"

Phil shrugged. "Yeah. Maybe."

The sergeant said, "Can you describe him?"

"He's handsome. Muscular, but not too muscular like a bodybuilder with the rippling veins and stuff. His forearms, though. Oh. He was in a suit. An ill-fitting suit because of the… you know… aforementioned muscles."

Phil rolled his eyes and mumbled, "Aforementioned?"

Kate added, "He's got a smile that lights up a room. And twinkly eyes. I can't believe I didn't recognize him when I saw him. But come on. He was in a Santa suit the first time... the hat, the beard, the whole nine yards. If you take off the suit, he's really handsome. Not that I undressed him or anything."

The sergeant said, "Rossi. I'm not seeing anyone on here with that name." Sergeant Campbell added, "I really wish someone like that came in here."

Natalie and Barbara walked over to the front desk.

Phil turned to them and said, "Rossi, right?"

Natalie said, "Yes. Rossi." Natalie spelled it for the sergeant.

The sergeant typed the name into the database search box. The computer made a noise. Sergeant Campbell looked up at them.

"I'm sorry, but I don't have anyone here by that name."

Natalie said, "But that's impossible. You guys lost my brother?"

Kate sighed and said, "This is like my luggage all over again." She paused and added, "Maybe he was sent to another police station?"

Sergeant Campbell said, "I'm searching the statewide database."

Officers Dwayne Wagner and Bill Ford came into the station. Kate looked at them as they headed toward the closed door. They were off to the Christmas party.

Kate recognized them. She blurted, "Wait. Those guys. Those guys are the ones who took him."

Wagner and Ford looked at each other. They noticed Barbara right away and whispered to one another.

Sergeant Campbell turned to them and said, "Wagner? Ford? What's going on?"

Wagner looked reluctant to speak. He went up to Sergeant Campbell and whispered in her ear.

"I see," Sergeant Campbell said gravely.

She turned back to Natalie, Kate, Barbara, and Phil.

"The incident involving Anthony Rossi was dismissed. The officers...drove Mr. Rossi home believing he was innocent of the charges brought against him."

Phil turned to the officers and said, "Did you watch the video?"

Wagner and Ford started to giggle...then...guffaw.

Wagner said, "Oh my God. When Marty goes flying into the Christmas tree. I watched it, like, four times. I hate that guy."

Ford nudged his fellow officer.

Wagner said, "I mean... There was video evidence that Mr. Rossi was not culpable of the crime he was alleged to have committed."

Sergeant Campbell asked, "What is this? What is going on?"

Wagner leaned over, with his cell phone in hand, and pressed the play button.

Sergeant Campbell said, "I saw this on the news the other day."

Natalie put her hand over her face.

Barbara peered at the screen, pointed, and said, "That one. That idiot is my husband."

Natalie leaned in and said, "That one is my little brother."

Kate turned to Wagner and Ford and said, "Wait. What did you do with him then?"

Wagner said, "We dropped him off at the home of..."

He looked at his notes and added, "Natalie Focareta."

Natalie corrected, "Rossi."

Barbara touched her arm, gently, kindly.

Natalie smiled and said, "Oh, thank God. He's not in the slammer."

Officer Wagner seemed to take umbrage at the word "slammer" but said nothing. The expression on his face was clear enough.

Officer Ford handed her a manila envelope.

Wagner said, "He left this. I found it in our back passenger seat. It must have fallen out of those ridiculously tight pants he was wearing."

Natalie took the envelope and saw his cell phone inside. "It was my husband's suit."

Wagner turned to Sergeant Campbell and said, "Thighs like tree trunks."

Sergeant Campbell said, "I kinda wish you would have brought him in. I have to stare at you goons all day."

Officer Ford rolled his eyes.

Natalie said, "Can we go?"

Sergeant Campbell said, "Yes. Unless you want to lodge a complaint against this guy in the video."

Wagner and Ford tried to stop Sergeant Campbell from finishing her sentence, but it was too late. She kept going. Sergeant Campbell added, "The one who attacked Rossi. You want to file a complaint against him?"

Everyone turned and looked at Barbara.

Barbara said, "Can I?"

Firefly in the Ointment

A few minutes later, Kate, Natalie, Barbara, and Phil stood outside in the parking lot.

Natalie turned to Barbara and said, "I'll take you home." She turned back to Kate and Phil. "Thank you so much for coming along with me. You didn't have to do that."

She spoke mostly to Phil, and it was pissing Kate off because he really didn't do anything but drive.

Natalie said to Phil, "You know, I've seen you before."

Phil smiled and said, "You have?"

Natalie added, "Yes. You were my UPS man. You used to deliver to my office. When I was at Wooten and Douglas."

Phil smiled and said, "FedEx. Wooten and Douglas was on my route. That was like ten years ago."

Natalie said, "I know. It was before I had the girls."

Phil said, "And you remembered me?"

Natalie said, "Are you kidding? I think I ordered some stuff on Amazon just so you could come by. I got the entire *Twilight Zone* collection sent to the office."

"I have that same box set," Phil said. "What's your favorite episode?"

"That's like picking my favorite kid. I can't choose. Everyone talks about the famous guest star ones, like 'Time, Enough at Last,' or 'Nightmare at Twenty-Thousand Feet,' but I like 'The Gift.' It's kind of like 'The Day the Earth Stood Still' with a darker ending."

"Wow. Obscure but interesting choice. I'm totally in it for the guest stars. I loved the Agnes Moorehead episode, and that creepy one with Billy Mumy."

"Those are great. 'The Invaders' and 'A Good Life.' Nice choices."

"Sadly, I don't know them by name like you do."

Kate was surprised. She assumed her cousin had encyclopedic knowledge of all things sci-fi. She said, "She's like a walking Wikipedia."

Phil realized that he had been monopolizing the conversation. He turned and looked at Kate and Barbara and said, "Oh, right. We should get going."

Phil pressed the button on his key fob, unlocking the car doors. Kate slid into the passenger seat.

Once he was in the driver's seat, he sighed.

"What?"

Phil turned to her and said, "Should we go back to the ball? I mean, I bet everyone is still dancing. And there was a wine basket I bid on in the silent auction."

Kate stared at him for a long moment.

She said, "Can you take me home? I think I've had enough excitement for one night."

Phil revved the engine. He turned back to Kate and said, "That Natalie Rossi is really something. What do you think the window is for a hot mom like that?"

"Pardon?"

Phil explained, "It's probably too early to ask her out, but if I wait too long, some other dude is going to snatch her up."

Kate put her head in her hands. She was exasperated, but he kept staring at her, the car still idling in the police station parking lot.

"Phil, I don't know. I. Don't. Know."

He retorted, "Why are you so pissed?"

Kate shrugged and said, "I don't know."

After another unbearably long pause, she said, "I'm sorry."

Kate didn't understand why she was angry.

Throw Pillows

Tony was sitting on the sofa flipping through a magazine when Natalie entered. She jumped back to see him in the living room, sitting on the sofa with Riley in his lap. He looked up at her and said, "I came home and there was no one here."

Natalie said, "I got a call from Marilyn. She took the kids to see *The Wizard of Oz*. It's playing at the Regent. She wanted them to see it on the big screen. The kids are going to sleep over at their house tonight." Natalie added, "I kinda feel bad though. Marie is not going to sleep after she sees those damn flying monkeys."

"Everyone is afraid of those damn things."

"Even you, soldier boy?"

"When I was, like, five. Hell yeah."

Natalie placed her award on the credenza and then collapsed onto the sofa next to him. She sighed. Natalie scratched Riley's head. The dog's eyes rolled back and then closed altogether.

"Did you have a key?"

"Nope."

"How did you get in?"

"Your bedroom window was slightly open."

"My bedroom is on the second floor."

"Nat, if I can get onboard a tanker that's been taken over by Somali pirates, I can get into a suburban house on St. Catherine Street."

Natalie tossed him a sly sideways glance and said, "Point."

Tony shifted in his seat. He stood up, paced around the room, looked out the curtains, and turned back to her.

Natalie looked up at him and said, "I know what you're doing. You are working your way up to an apology. You don't have to."

He smiled and said, "Good." He plopped back down on the sofa.

Natalie grabbed a pillow and swatted him with it.

"I really am sorry," he said after a moment. "I wanted to give you a perfect Christmas."

Natalie looked over at him and said, "It's not."

He looked hurt, but Natalie laughed.

He took the pillow and swatted her back. Riley growled.

Natalie turned to the dog and said, "Good boy. You're finally on *my* side."

The dog stared at her and, once again, cocked his furry black head.

Natalie turned back to her brother and said, "This is not your fault. Looking back, I realize I should have never dragged you to see Santa while you were *dressed* as Santa." She thought for a moment and said, "That sounds really stupid out loud."

Tony said, "You should have heard it over here."

She reached for the pillow, but Tony grabbed her arm. Tony said, "That's not why they call them 'throw pillows,' you know."

They both laughed.

Greetings from Abroad

Mid-afternoon the next day, Kate was in the laundry room, folding her very few clothes. She was running around the house in her panties and bra, even though it was chilly in the large Victorian. She heard her cell phone ring and ran upstairs to chase after the noise. It was in the kitchen on the counter next to a neat stack of dish towels she had laundered earlier. When Kate picked it up, she heard her mother's voice.

"Kate. Greetings from—wait—Drew, where are we?"

Drew chimed in, "Greetings from...somewhere in the Caribbean."

Her mom and brother were trying to share a cell phone. They were calling from the boat, somewhere in the middle of the ocean. The call was half static.

Virginia laughed, "Oh that's right. It's pretty much water. Water as far as the eye can see. 'Water, water, everywhere and not a drop to drink.' Well now. Who said that? Byron? Tennyson? F. Scott Fitzgerald?"

Kate answered, "Coleridge. Samuel Taylor Coleridge."

Virginia giggled. "I knew it was someone with three names. Like Jonathan Taylor Thomas."

Drew grabbed the phone and said, "She's drunk."

Virginia grabbed it back and shouted into the phone, "Shush. I had a couple of Penis Coladas."

Kate said, "Um. You mean Pina Coladas."

Virginia replied, "No. Yes. Well, sort of. It's a Pina Colada in a large plastic cup shaped liked a ding-dong."

Drew and Virginia howled with laughter.

Kate said, "I thought this was a family cruise."

Drew blurted, "The kids aren't allowed in this area."

Virginia said, "Wait. Wait. I'll text you a picture. Drew. Drew. Show me how to do this text-a-picture thing."

Drew responded, "Not now. We're in the middle of a phone conversation with Kate."

Kate said, "Are we, though?"

Kate felt like the third person in a two-person improv scene, like an extra in her own movie.

"Kitty has claws," Drew said under his breath.

Kate coldly said, "Merry Christmas, Andrew."

He hated being called Andrew, as much as Kate hated being called Kitty, a nickname Drew successfully launched for her in grade school. She didn't escape the nickname until she got to Northwestern.

With a sudden burst of joy, Drew said, "Merry Christmas, big sis."

Kate waited a beat for Virginia to jump in, but there was only silence and static on her cell phone.

Kate asked, "What happened to Mom?"

Drew started laughing.

"Drew?"

"She passed out on the deck chair. Like just now. It's hilarious. She still has her 'Penis Colada' in her hand. I *will* be texting you a pic."

Kate sighed and said, "So you guys are having a good time, then?"

"The best. I mean... I wish Connor was here but, otherwise, we're having a blast."

That stung. Of course, Drew wanted his husband along for the trip, but it hurt to hear he wanted Connor there...and not her. Kate said nothing.

After a long uncomfortable moment, Drew said, "Roaming charges and stuff. I still have to call the hubster. He finished his project yesterday and he's getting to spend the holidays in Sausalito with his parental units."

Kate wanted to say, "I didn't ask," but refrained. Instead she offered up another, slightly more cheerful, "Merry Christmas. Tell Connor I said Merry Christmas and all the shit that goes with it."

"Yeah. Will do. Merry Christmas, sis. I love you. Miss you."

He hung up, and there was a sudden silence. The house felt big and empty. The phone buzzed once more. She looked down at it. Drew, true to his word, sent a picture of their mother passed out in a deck chair; a straw hat covered most of her face, and she was wearing a tasteful, blue one-piece with a gauzy, white linen cover-up. Clasped to her hand, even while unconscious, was a large pink, plastic cup that looked like a hollow dildo with a straw hanging out of the urethra like a red and white striped catheter. Kate offered up a wistful smile.

For some reason, she began to cry.

Conversations with my Father

In the early evening, Kate called her father. She mustered up the strength to say, "Merry Christmas," but it all fell apart soon after a brief conversation about the weather.

After a few minutes of idle chitchat, her father said, "Sweetie, put your mom on the phone. I better wish her a Merry Christmas or I'll never hear the end of it."

"She's not here."

It wasn't until that moment Kate realized that she was feeling lonely, abandoned. All the emotions she had been repressing bubbled to the surface. Her happy-go-lucky façade cracked.

"Okay. Is Andrew around?"

That's when a small tear rolled down Kate's left cheek. She wiped it away with her hand, but another tear followed. The floodgates were open.

Kate unloaded it all. "Dad, they went on a cruise. I'm in Mom's house alone. I lost my tooth, and you won't believe what I went through to get it back. And, yeah, and I lost my job."

There was a long silence. Kate covered her mouth. She didn't make a sound, but the tears still flowed.

Finally, her father asked, "Do you need money?"

"No. I'm fine. I'll be fine. That's not it. I was just hoping to have a nice little Christmas, and it all went to shit."

"Language."

"Dad. Seriously? I wanted this perfect Christmas and I got this…this…whatever this festering pile of—doggy doo-doo. There, happy?"

Her father laughed. She couldn't see him, but knew he nodded and then said, "A perfect Christmas? Kate-bug, there is no such thing as a perfect Christmas."

"Yeah. Perfect. Like the ones we had growing up."

"You thought those were perfect?"

Kate smiled. She waxed nostalgic for her childhood Christmases.

Her dad said, "You remember the year I got laid off and we almost didn't have a Christmas at all? If the Kleins hadn't paid me to saw a pine down in their backyard, we wouldn't have had a tree. You can thank root rot for that."

"We strung it up with popcorn we sewed together on a string."

"Yeah. It was a lot cheaper than lights and it saved on the electric bill."

Kate insisted, "That was the best Christmas. You took us sledding every day of our school break."

"Because I didn't have a job."

"We sang Christmas carols."

"Because I had the cable TV shut off. I had to keep you kids entertained."

"I got Mystery Date for Christmas. Drew got Rock 'em, Sock 'em Robots."

"Honey, I got Mystery Date from the Goodwill, and those robots were mine. I had them growing up. Basically, I went Christmas shopping in my mom's attic. You didn't notice the masking tape on the yellow robot's leg? They don't come out of the box like that."

"Drew always got up super early on Christmas morning. I thought he broke it before I woke up and came downstairs. Besides, we loved Rock 'em, Sock 'em Robots. It turned out that Drew liked playing Mystery Date more than I did."

"I ignored all the clues."

"That was a great Christmas."

Kate remembered, "We got Operation, too."

"Also from your nana's attic. You spent more time fighting over the cardboard box it came in."

Kate laughed and said, "I was heavily into my diorama period."

"I remember. That was the year all my shoeboxes disappeared, including the one I kept my receipts in. I had to listen to a thirty-minute lecture from Herb, my tax guy, about the importance of backing up my claims."

"If it's any consolation, McClellan fought back Robert E. Lee in that shoebox."

"The battle of Antietam took six percent of my gross that year. I was lucky I was working again by mid-January."

Kate smiled and said, "It was a good year."

There was another long pause. And her father queried, "Don't you remember your mom and me yelling at each other?"

"Drew and I were always yelling at each other, too. I just thought that's what people did."

"You were kids. And I guess so were we. Your mom and me, I mean. Neither of us were ready for all the responsibility. We did the best we could, though."

Kate said, "And it was great."

Her father added, "But it was never perfect."

They continued to talk about many things, but for Kate nothing was as impactful as this revelation that her childhood Christmases were messier than she had remembered them. She was buoyant knowing she didn't have to work quite so hard making sure everything was perfect.

Unexpected Company

Kate plugged her phone back into her charger. She looked up at the clock in the kitchen and realized it was time to get ready for her cousin's Christmas party. Her conversation with her father revived her joy de vivre.

The phone rang again. She assumed her father forgot to tell her something and picked it back up without looking at the number.

"I'm in your neighborhood and coming to your house."

The voice belonged to her former boss, Matt Zimmerman.

Kate responded, "Matt? I'm not home. I'm in Connecticut."

"Yes. That's what I mean. Connecticut. I'll be there in—hang on." There was a slight pause. "The driver said, and I quote, 'We'll be there by six-twenty, my friend.' Isn't that lovely? We've only said seven words to each other and we're friends already. Who said New Yorkers weren't friendly?"

"Matt, what's going on?"

"I was in the city for a meeting. I'm going to be doing a segment for ABC's *New Year's Rockin' Eve*. Stan gave me your mom's address."

Stan was Kate's agent.

"Um. Okay. That's cool."

Matt added, "I want to talk to you. In person."

"Okay. But if you're coming here, you're coming to my cousin's house for a Christmas party."

"You gentiles and the Christmas. Okay. I should stop and get something. Wine, flowers... cocaine?"

"Just bring yourself, you idiot."

"Almost there. Oh. This town is so quaint. It's like you were born in a Hallmark movie."

***

A few minutes later, Matt Zimmerman stood in the doorway. He was tall and lanky with a boyish face that seemed to be incapable of growing a beard. Kate used to call him "The World's Tallest Baby."

Kate came to the door in the other new dress she had bought at the mall. Unfortunately, she wasn't all the way in it.

She said, "Good. You're here. You can zip me up."

"Usually when I show up, women take their clothes off."

Kate retorted, "For cash and prizes."

"Touché."

Matt zipped up her dress.

"Matt, I don't mean to be rude, but why are you here?"

"You'll be proud of me. I've been hustling since the cancelation. Actually, I was hustling since we got our first jeer in *TV Guide*. I have been talking to agents, managers, producers, and production companies. Everyone. Cutting to the chase: the network is giving me a late-night talk show."

"That's great. You won't have to act."

"Ouch, sweetie. Ouch."

"I'm sorry. But the whole time I've been saying—"

Matt and Kate said, in unison, "'You need to be more yourself.'"

Matt continued, "Yeah. Yeah. I know. Anyway, I need a head writer."

"Doug isn't going to do it?"

"Doug got a development deal with HBO, like, today. He's out. I need you, Kate."

"Wow. I guess everyone was hustling while I've been floundering around in suburbia."

"You gonna be my head writer or what? Don't worry. Just because the title is head writer, it doesn't mean you'll be on your knees the whole time."

"Matthew. I was going to give you a hug, but you made it awkward."

He smiled and said, "That's my thing."

They smiled at one another. She hugged him. It was a warm, affectionate moment.

In mid-hug she said, "Wait. You came all the way to tell me this in person?"

Matt kept a firm grip on her.

"Don't be mad. But I think Doug wanted you for his HBO thing. I wanted to scoop you up before he got to you. If I get a blurb out in *Variety* this week, he won't ask you. I bet HBO pays more."

She swatted at him playfully.

"Smooth move, dickhead."

He pleaded, "Kate. Please. Pretty please."

"I'll go with you." She paused and added, "Unless Dougie offers me a crap-load of moolah."

Zimmerman looked hurt.

"Oh, come on. I'm teasing. I'm super excited."

She hugged him again.

Matt pushed her off and joked, "Okay. Okay. I can't be caught fraternizing with my employees."

Kate noticed the time and said, "We're going to be late."

Matt queried, "Where are we going again?"

"My cousin's Christmas party. I have to put it in my map thingie on my phone. I've only been there once before. If I can get us to St. Catherine Street, we should be fine."

"St. Catherine Street? Will I be the only Jewish-slash-Buddhist comedian there?"

"I'm not gonna lie. It's gonna be ninety-nine point nine percent WASP. This is Connecticut. The Protestants landed in Plymouth Rock and never left the Eastern seaboard. My family was treated like outcasts because we were half-Irish, for God's sake. You'll be a circus freak there. That's why I can't wait to take you."

Matt deadpanned, "Oh joy."

When they stood out on the porch, Matt tripped over a suitcase. "Who leaves a suitcase on the porch?"

Kate looked at it, incredulous. "Was that here when you showed up just now?"

"Yeah, I guess."

"Oh my God. Oh my God."

She got down and hugged the suitcase. Matt stared at her.

"Sweetie, are you okay?"

Kate said to the suitcase, "I missed you so much."
"Should I leave you two alone?"

Fancy Footwork

Tony asked, "Where are we going again?"

Natalie was zipping up Marie's left boot. "I know. This is a lot of work to go across the street, but I promised them I'd pop in. The girls love playing with their toddler."

Danielle was standing by the door in her coat. "Can we just go?"

Natalie shot back, "Does it look like we can go?"

Marie had only one boot on.

Danielle said, "She can hop."

Natalie glared at her.

Tony said, "Maybe I should hang here and watch the dog."

"Riley will be fine."

Riley looked up at Tony. Clearly, the Scottie disagreed with her.

Natalie paused while pushing Marie's little foot into her other boot. She said, "Actually, he'll need a walk in about an hour. If you're not having a good time, you can come back and do that."

Danielle said, "Make sure he does his 'business.' That's code for poop."

Marie covered her mouth and giggled.

Natalie looked up at Marie's bare hands. "Wait. Where are your gloves? I just put those pink gloves on your hands a second ago."

Marie shrugged and said, "I don't know."

Danielle sat down in the foyer and huffed loudly. She barked, "We are never leaving here."

Natalie turned to Tony and said, "You still want to have a family?"

Charades

St. Catherine Street was lined with cars. Kate parked the car as close to the house as she could, but it was still some distance. Matt burst out of the passenger side door.

Kate opened up her door and got out. Matt was holding his abdomen. She turned to him and said, "You should have gone at my house. Go. I'll get the presents."

As Kate grabbed two large shopping bags filled with gifts from the trunk of the car, she watched Matt run for the front door.

Gwen answered the door, gasped, and shut it again. Matt turned back to Kate and shrugged.

From behind the door, even Kate could hear Gwen say, "Oh my God. Matt Zimmerman is knocking on my door."

Matt yelled back, "He is. And if you don't open up, he's gonna pee in your mailbox."

By the time Gwen reopened the door, Kate had joined Matt on the porch.

Kate said, "Hey, cuz, I brought a friend. Can you take him on a tour of the house starting with a bathroom?"

Gwen ushered the TV celebrity to the nearest bathroom. Kate entered. She greeted a room full of people. She dropped the bags by the big, beautiful Christmas tree in the living room.

Gwen's husband, Ed, came in for a hug. After a firm embrace, he helped her out of her coat and walked her toward the bar. The jovial host slung the coat over his arm and said, "Let's get you a big girl drink. Ask for a Christmas Peppermint Stick. It's got peppermint schnapps, berry vodka, and some kinda chocolate flavoring."

The bartender said, "Crème de cacao."

The drink was served with a small peppermint stick in it. Kate slid the concoction back to the bartender, turned to her cousin-in-law, and said, "Maybe later. Where's Aunt Vi?"

Ed nodded toward the kitchen.

***

Kate found Violet rinsing dishes. Even though Gwen had hired a catering company, complete with a chef, cater-waiters, and a cleanup crew, Violet insisted on helping out.

Kate and Violet embraced. It was a little awkward, because Violet's hands were wet and she held them out away from Kate's new dress so she wouldn't get soap suds on them.

Gwen sauntered through the kitchen doorway and said, "Maybe you can convince her to come out to the party instead of hiding in the kitchen."

Kate and Gwen hugged. Gwen whispered in her ear, "Seriously though. Matt Zimmerman?"

"He's a friend."

Violet dried her hands with a towel and said, "I want to check on Dax."

"I invited some neighbor kids to play with him. They're all running around in the game room downstairs."

Violet said, "I'm just going to look in on them."

Violet exited the kitchen.

Kate turned to Gwen and said, "You know my mom is the same way."

"Yeah, except Aunt Vir is on a cruise with Drew. That's awesome. I could never get Mom on a cruise."

"It's a little weird, though, right? You know it's a gay cruise?"

Gwen shrugged. "I think it's great. Your mom needs to loosen up. Have fun."

"Trust me. She is. Have you not heard about The Ladies Night Incident?"

Gwen looked at her.

Violet returned to the kitchen and said, "Kate, can I see you for a moment?"

"Sorry. I assumed Gwen knew about my mom's DUI."

Violet said, "She does now. But that's not it. Come with me." Violet took Kate aside. She whispered, "The *In Bradbury* dentist is here. With his wife."

Kate gasped. Gwen, however, still heard them.

Gwen said, "You guys know Dr. Schultheiss? He and Caroline live down the street. We met them at the block party this summer. I'm glad they're here together. I heard they were—" Gwen whispered, "—going through a rough patch."

Matt popped his head into the kitchen. The cater-waiters looked up from their tasks as he entered the kitchen, but their boss, Midge, a short, thin woman with large rimmed glasses, scowled at them and they returned to work.

Matt said, "You left me out in the hive, Kate."

Kate replied, "Wasps have nests, bees have hives."

"I'm getting hives being in a room full of people I don't know."

Kate turned to Gwen and Violet and said, "Comedians. You can put them on stage in front of a hundred people, but you can't leave them alone at a party."

Matt agreed. He added, "It's better on stage, Kate. No one talks back."

"If you're lucky."

Kate grabbed Matt by the arm and led him past Gwen, Violet, and the swarm of cater-waiters.

"I need to see you for a second."

They sequestered themselves in the pantry, a nook off the kitchen filled with groceries.

"I need a favor."

"Another one?"

"There's a guy here, Herman Schultheiss, DDS. He is here…with his wife. I need you to pretend to be my boyfriend."

"Didn't we do this bit in episode three? It didn't work out for me on the show."

"Can you just do this?"

"What's my motivation?"

"I'm hot and you're lucky."

"It'll be the acting job of the century."

Kate punched him in the arm.

"Ow. Okay. What's my character?"

"You're you. Just don't be as much you… as you usually are."

Kate swung the pantry door wide open and they walked through the kitchen arm in arm.

Matt turned to Violet and Gwen and said, "We're dating now," but used air quotes when he said "dating."

Kate elbowed him. She murmured, "Watch it with the air quotes," out of the side of her mouth.

Gwen smiled and said, "That's terrific."

Violet leaned over to Gwen and whispered, "Sweetie, they're faking."

Gwen said, "What's happening? Why is Kate making my Christmas party weird?"

Close Encounters

Kate and Matt held hands when they ran into Dr. Herman Schultheiss and his wife.

The dentist said, "Hello there."

Kate gripped Matt's hand even harder.

"Kate, this is my wife, Caroline. Caroline, this is a…new patient of mine."

"Yes. And this is my boyfriend, Matt. He flew in from Los Angeles to surprise me. Isn't that terrific?"

Matt repeated, "Why yes. I did fly in from Los Angeles to surprise her."

So far, Kate was sticking as close to the truth as she could, but she wanted to kick Matt in the shin for his performance as "the boyfriend." It was yet another awful acting job.

Caroline was an attractive redhead with a short crop of hair.

The doctor's wife turned to Matt and said, "I've seen you on television. I don't remember your name, though. Is it Chuck something?"

"Chuck? Do I look like a Chuck? Come on, Caroline, Kate said my name like two seconds ago."

Herman said to Caroline, "Kate is a writer for *The Matt Zimmerman Show*. And this young man is—"

Matt prompted, "Don't tell her." He paused and said, "Come on, Caroline. You got this."

Caroline stitched it together slowly, and stuttered, "Is… Matt Zimmerman."

"Yes. You've won a year's supply of Turtle Wax."

"I did?"

Herman said, "Honey, the comedian is making fun of you."

Matt scoffed, "Hermie—that was harsh."

Dr. Schultheiss stared at Matt curiously. Matt could see his tongue move around in his mouth, pushing against his cheek.

Dr. Schultheiss said, "How did you know my name? I didn't say it."

Kate jumped in, "I told him all about my emergency visit to the dentist, Dr. Schultheiss."

Schultheiss laughed nervously. He said, "It was quite humorous. She came in with coffee all over her clothes and no front tooth. She was a mess. You should have seen her."

"I collided with a guy on Front Street. It was horrible."

Caroline inquired, "Oh my. How's your car?"

"No. We smashed into each other on the street. Pedestrian collision. He was dressed like Santa Claus."

Matt slowly turned to her and whispered, "I thought we weren't improvising this bit."

"No. He really was dressed like Santa Claus." Kate added, "There was a dog, too."

Matt pleaded, "Stop." The comedian doubled over with laughter. Matt choked out, "Dressed like Santa Claus."

Kate said, "Not the dog, too. Just the guy."

Matt had a robust laugh. It was contagious. Everyone in listening range started to laugh, except Schultheiss. The dentist's facial features hardened. He was stoic. George Washington on Mount Rushmore.

Herman looked straight at Kate and said, "So, you told him all about me."

Kate winked. "Maybe not all."

The dentist took a sip of his cocktail. The peppermint stick in the martini glass pushed up against the side of his nose.

Kate grabbed Matt's hand and said, "That looks delicious. Let's go get a drink. Nice seeing you again, Doctor."

Matt was still laughing as Kate pulled him away.

Caroline shouted, "Nice meeting you, Chuck."

Who Let the Dogs Out

Ed opened the front door and greeted Natalie, Tony, and the girls. Danielle and Marie ran to the game room door. Danielle looked back at Natalie before opening it.

Natalie sighed and said, "Go on."

With that, the girls charged down the steps and out of sight.

Ed looked at Natalie and smiled. He was in his early forties with a pleasant smile and a slight paunch, salt-and-pepper hair, and a ruddy complexion.

"Natalie," Ed exclaimed. "I'm glad you could make it. I bet you could use a drink. And you, too, big fella."

"This is my brother, Anthony."

"Tony," he insisted.

Ed shook Tony's hand vigorously, patted both of them on the back, and corralled them toward the bar. He added, "Let's get you two a drink."

Ed led them to the bar. Tony noticed a man staring at his sister from across the room.

Tony whispered to his sister, "Creeper on your ten."

Natalie glanced about. She spotted him hovering around the Christmas tree.

She queried, "Phil?"

Phil smiled and strolled over to them.

Phil joked, "I see you found our missing Santa Claus."

Natalie laughed. Tony thought his sister laughed a little too hard.

There was a moment of silence and Natalie said, "Phil, this is my brother Tony. Tony, this is Phil. He came to my rescue when you were hauled off and carted away at the Christmas ball."

"I see."

Ed grabbed Tony and swung him around. "Tony, I want you to meet my wife, Gwen."

Gwen was much younger than her husband. She was a little stout, but she had naturally curly hair and an infectious smile. Standing so near her brother Phil, Tony could see a resemblance. Gwen and Phil had a lot of similar features: big smiles, dimples, and thick eyebrows—though, of course, Gwen's were delicately contoured.

Gwen remarked to Tony, "My goodness. You look like a movie star."

Ed joked, "Ha. We already have one of those here."

Gwen corrected, "I think he's just a TV star, but I'll have to Google him."

Tony said, "I'm sorry. I'm not following this conversation."

Ed roared, "Matt Zimmerman is in the house."

Ed had been ushering everyone to the bar as they arrived at the party. It was eight-thirty and he was already drunk. He sounded like a frat boy.

Gwen explained, "Kate works on his show."

"Kate?"

Gwen said, "Kate. My cousin. You have to meet her."

Gwen pointed to Kate and Matt. They were in the dining room, a few yards away. A teenager was posing with the two of them for a picture on his phone. The boy extended his arm as far as he could as he tried to cram all three of their heads into one picture for the selfie. The teenager snapped a few photos. Then he vigorously shook Matt's hand. Kate ushered Matt away from his biggest fan. They walked toward the bar.

When Tony spied her from across the room, he got a bit of a jolt. It was the girl he was most eager to see, but then he noticed that Matt and Kate were holding hands. His heart sank.

Tony turned to Natalie, who was jabbering on to Phil about the sociopolitical commentary of *Star Trek* and its effect on modern science fiction.

Tony said, "I'm gonna go let the dog out."

Natalie exclaimed, "But we just got here."

Phil barked. He merrily sang several choruses of "Who let the dogs out?"

Phil was also, clearly, tipsy.

Tony turned back to Gwen and Ed and said, "Excuse me."

He walked out the front door.

New Choice

Kate was walking through the party holding Matt's hand, avoiding Herman and/or Caroline Schultheiss. Across the room, she spotted Tony Rossi. She immediately disengaged her hand from her faux beau, but it was too late.

She watched Tony turn to Natalie and Phil, say a few words, and then bolt for the front door.

She froze. She had no idea what to do next. It seemed odd to chase after him; after all, he was relatively a stranger. However, it seemed stranger to ignore him or let him get away. Her hesitation cost her critical seconds. By the time she worked her way through the crowd, he was gone.

She wandered over to the bar where Matt had sidled up to Natalie and Phil.

Matt smiled and said, "I'm Matt Zimmerman and this is my girlfriend, Kate."

Kate pushed her way through the crowd and said, "Um. No."

Matt misunderstood her denial. He exclaimed, "I'm Matt Zimmerman and this is Lady Elizabeth Cottswald of Downington on the Hartfordshire."

"No. Matt. We're not—"

"I'm Matt Zimmerman and this is Betty Lou Puckett from Slip-in-the-Mud, Arkansas."

"Matt, stop."

"You said I had to be me, but you didn't say you had to be you." Matt whispered, "Come on. Play along. It's been a while since I heard your Southern accent."

"Matt, I know these people."

"Oh. Right."

Kate explained, "This is my cousin Phil and this is—"

She didn't quite know how to introduce her new friend. But Natalie stuck out her hand to Matt and said, "I'm Natalie. I live across the street there."

Natalie pointed to the big bay window in front of them. Her house was directly across the road.

Kate said, "There? This whole time you lived across the street from Gwen?"

Phil poked his head between Kate and Natalie and said, "Isn't that freaking awesome?"

Kate got a whiff of Phil's breath and said, "You might want to lay off the signature cocktail, Phil. You smell like the inside of a York Peppermint Patty."

Phil cupped his hand over his mouth, blew into it, and held it up to his nose.

Kate said, "Gimme a minute. I need to talk to Natalie." And she pulled Natalie aside.

They moved a few feet away from Matt and Phil. Kate looked over at Matt and back to Natalie and said, "He's not my boyfriend."

Natalie whispered, "Good. He's weirder in person than he is on TV."

"I need to talk to your brother."

"Okay. He went to take Riley for a walk."

Kate marched upstairs to the guest bedroom and grabbed her coat from a pile on the bed, descended the staircase, and ran into Gwen midway. Her cousin was carrying two more coats upstairs. They met on the landing.

Gwen asked, "Where are you going?"

"I'm taking the dog for a walk. I'll be right back."

Kate bounced down the remaining steps and shot out the front door. As Gwen watched her depart, she yelled, "But you don't have a dog."

Together

When Tony grabbed the leash from a hook on the wall, Riley went crazy. He jumped about, spun around in the air, and landed. Tony clipped the leash on and opened the door.

Kate stood underneath the lintel. She was poised to knock but Tony had opened the door seconds before her fist rapped on it. Her hand was inches away from his nose.

Kate squeaked, "Um, hi."

They looked at each other for a long time. It was the most awkward pause in the history of awkward pauses.

He couldn't help himself; he broke the tension by asking, "Why are you here?"

Kate scratched the top of her head and said, "I'm not sure." She looked back over at Gwen's house and then looked back at him. "I was hoping you'd come back to the party. I brought a tray of my mom's cookies. Actually, my aunt Violet brought them, but I gave them to her the night we… um… met."

Tony patted his flat stomach and replied, "I don't really do sugar."

"Oh. Right. I just thought you'd want to taste them. You know, since the dog here already has."

Tony laughed. Riley was sitting beside him, panting in anticipation of his walk around the neighborhood.

"You do remember me then?"

"Not fair. I met you in a Santa suit. To be honest, when you were at the gym I had no idea who you were. And then at the—"

"Don't say it."

"Ball?"

Riley ran around in circles, twisting the leash around Tony's legs. Tony tried to hop out of his entanglements but had to lean on Kate's shoulder to free himself. She helped steady him.

"Fascinating."

"Just don't say that word."

"Ball?"

On cue, Riley went nuts again.

There was a long silence between them once Riley calmed.

Finally, Kate said, "I came to apologize mostly. And I wanted you to know that Matt Zimmerman is not my boyfriend."

"I don't—I mean, who you date is your—I don't know who that is."

"The guy in there…" Kate pointed back to her cousin's house. "He's my boss."

"That makes it even weirder."

Kate said it out loud, "I was holding hands with my boss. You're right. That does make it weirder."

She smiled, and Tony couldn't resist. He smiled back. "I see you got that tooth fixed."

"Yes. It looks like the original. See." She babbled, "I lost the original in eleventh grade, but it looked like the last one, which was also fake, by the way. But that one looked like the original. So, there you have it. This is too much. I'm talking too much."

Tony could not help but continue to smile at her. It was a big, goofy smile. "You're cute."

Kate squirmed. "I might have been the one who got you arrested," she blurted out.

Tony laughed.

"I sort of outed you to Marty What's-his-Name."

"Marty What's-his-Name? Kasiewicz?"

"Yes. I think that's it. Barb's husband."

"You did that?"

"Not intentionally. Here's the thing, we were at the—"

Tony held his index finger over his mouth, trying to shush her.

Kate looked down at the dog. "The place." She added, "Reminds me of an old *All in the Family* bit about yellow cling peaches. 'Hmmm hmmm hmmm…in heavy syrup.'" Kate sighed and added, "I watched a lot of Nick at Nite growing up."

There was another awkward silence between them. Tony had never seen the old TV show and the reference was lost on him.

"I mentioned to Mr. and Mrs. Kazakhstan or whatever that you were Santa Claus when I met you. It sounded weird then and it sounds weird now."

"It *was* your fault."

"If it's any consolation. I feel terrible about it. We tried to free you from jail, but I guess the cops took pity on you and let you out— on your own recognizance, I guess. I wanted to apologize for all of that."

Tony grinned. "We could have danced together instead."

"At—" Kate glanced down at Riley who was staring up at her, panting. "The Christmas—mmm-hmmm."

Tony nodded. Kate backed away from him.

"I came over to apologize. So. Um. Mission accomplished."

They stood there, gawking at one another. After a long moment, Kate looked away.

"Did you do all of this?" She studied the lights around the eaves, framing the porch in multicolored bulbs. He could tell she was only feigning interest in the Christmas decorations.

"Natalie—my sister—did most of it."

Kate glanced up at a sprig of mistletoe above the entrance. She pointed to it and leaned in close.

Tony grabbed her and kissed her. Kate gasped against his lips before giving in to him, fully, freely. They held each other tight for a few long moments. Realizing they were smooching on his sister's front porch, Tony broke away. He looked around. No one was watching…except Riley.

"Do you want to come with me and Riley here on our—W-A-L-K?"

Kate nodded. "If I'm gonna hang out with you, I'm gonna need a list of words we can and cannot say in front of this dog."

"Gotcha."

Riley led the two down the street. By the time they reached the corner, Tony grabbed her hand. "Your hands are so cold," he said.

She replied, "Cold hands, warm heart."

He looked her in the eye and said, "Yeah. I can see that."

They cut through the park. Snow started to fall. They walked toward the gazebo in the center. Twinkling white lights were strewn about the canopy. There were two speakers mounted on the fret curves. The speakers played Christmas music.

Tony pushed a stray lock of hair out of her face and kissed her. Over the speakers, Johnny Mathis sang "Winter Wonderland."

Kate turned to him and said, "This is nice. Walking with you and Riley—in the same direction this time."

He smiled sheepishly. "With all of your teeth."

"I probably won't try to have you arrested again."

"Probably?"

"I can't promise anything."

This time, she was the one who pulled him in for a kiss.

Epilogue

The following Christmas, Kate stood at the luggage carousel at Bradley International Airport waiting on her bags. She held a small bundle tightly to her chest. A small baby girl slept underneath the soft pink blanket.

Her brother Drew stood next to her as he pulled a stroller from the conveyor belt. He assembled it with haste. Her brother's husband, Connor, came over to her and held his hands out. Kate handed the baby over to him.

"Here ya go, Emily. Back to Daddy." She paused then added, "Well, one of them."

Connor looked around at a pile of bags at their feet, softly rubbing Emily's back. "This seems to be all of it."

Drew replied, "Kate's bag didn't come off the thing yet."

Kate sighed. The baggage carousel was empty.

"Par for the course. I guess I'll go talk to the woman at the desk."

Kate turned to find the customer service rep as the machine belched. Several bags pushed their way out from behind the plastic strips and tumbled down the conveyor.

Kate cheered when she saw the beaten brown valise with a bright green bow attached to its handle.

"I can't believe it. My luggage decided to show up this Christmas."

It chugged along the conveyor with a few other assorted bags. Kate grabbed her bag and pulled it from the belt. She turned to Connor and said, "Did I tell you the airline rerouted my bag all over creation last year?"

Drew sidled up to her and said, "You told *everybody*."

A man dressed like Santa Claus approached. He had a small bag from the gift shop.

Drew turned to Kate and said, "Why is your hubby dressed like Santa?"

"It's a thing. He's got this wacky new Christmas tradition."

Tony bellowed a hearty, "Ho-ho-ho."

Kate looked at Connor and Drew and said, "That's one ho for each of us."

Drew whispered, "Speak for yourself, hussy."

Tony pulled down his beard as he approached. He announced, "This thing is itchy."

Kate smiled and said, "No one's making you wear it, honey."

She pulled back at the beard and kissed him. Then, she snapped the beard back into place.

"Hey. Ow. And I went and bought you something."

He teased Kate with the plastic bag. She tried to reach it as he held it high over his head.

Drew said, "He's already exchanging gifts. At the airport, no less."

Tony relented and handed Kate the bag. "I found this at the newsstand on my way to the head."

Kate opened the bag and pulled out a *TV Guide*. The cover had a picture of Matt Zimmerman sitting at a big oak desk. The caption read "Get the inside scoop on 'Tonight with Matt Z.' Read our exclusive interview with head writer Kate Nolan-Rossi."

"It's out. I didn't realize it came out this week."

Drew said, "I need a copy."

The sliding glass doors opened and Virginia entered the airport. Snowflakes blew in with her. She flailed her arms about in an attempt to get their attention. Virginia yelled, "Come on. I'm in the white zone. I'm not supposed to leave the car."

Connor strapped Emily into the stroller. The baby fussed a little but wiggled into a comfortable position and fell back asleep.

Virginia joined them, completing the family reunion in Baggage Claim.

Drew whispered to Kate, "Check her breath. I don't want her driving my baby around if she's had...you know...a nip."

Kate hugged her mother and said, "Mom." She added, "I'll tell you what, gimme the keys. I'll run out and sit in the car and you can organize these slowpokes."

Drew mouthed "thank you" as Kate grabbed the keys from Virginia's hands. Kate turned back to him and whispered, "I think it's just the smell of vanilla from all the baking, but why take chances?"

She scurried toward the door, sidestepping the crowds of people waiting for friends, relatives, taxis, or super-shuttles to transport them home for the holidays. Kate took one final look back at her family before exiting into the cold Connecticut air. Virginia was dispensing a round of hugs to Drew, Connor, and Tony.

Kate knew it wouldn't be a perfect Christmas, but she had never been happier.

RECIPES

Tea-Time Tassies

Tea-Time Tassies are bite-size pecan pies.

Ingredients:

Pastry:
- 4 ounces cream cheese, softened
- ½ cup butter, softened
- 1 cup all-purpose flour

Filling:
- 1 egg
- ¾ cup brown sugar
- 1 Tablespoon butter, melted
- 1 teaspoon vanilla extract
- Dash salt
- 2/3 cup pecans, chopped

1. Cream together cream cheese and butter until smooth. Add in flour and mix until completely combined. Place dough in a covered container and refrigerate for at least 1 hour.

2. Roll dough into 1-inch balls and place in mini muffin tins. Press dough up sides of tin to create a shell (like a tiny pecan pie crust).

3. For the filling, beat egg well then add brown sugar, butter, vanilla, and salt. Mix again till well combined. Stir in pecans.

4. Spoon filling into prepared pastry-lined cups.

5. Bake in a preheated 325-degree oven for 25 minutes. Remove from oven and let cool completely before removing from tins.

Pizzelles

An Italian cookie that means "small, flat, and round." They look like hex signs on the side of Amish barns.

You need a special tool, a pizzelle iron, to make the cookies properly.

Ingredients:

• 4 ¾ cups of flour
• 1 ¾ cup of sugar
• 2 sticks of butter
• 1 or 2 teaspoons of anise oil
• 1 or 2 teaspoon vanilla extract
• 5 teaspoons of baking powder
• 7 eggs

1. Preheat pizzelle iron and lightly coat with nonstick cooking spray.
2. Melt two sticks (1/2 pound) of butter and let cool.
3. Beat 7 eggs into cool butter.
4. Add 1 ¾ cup of sugar gradually. Beat till fluffy.
5. 1 or 2 teaspoons of vanilla, and 1 or 2 teaspoons of anise oil. Mix in 5 level teaspoons of baking powder.
6. Add 4 ¾ cups of flour. Mix well.
7. Spoon on to pizzelle iron.
8. Press 20 seconds.
9. Cool and stack.
10. Makes around 6 dozen (first two may stick – depending on your iron). Lift with a spatula.
11. Sprinkle with powdered sugar (optional).

ABOUT THE AUTHOR

Mike Buzzelli is a standup comedian and sit-down author. As a comedian, he has performed all around the country, most notably, the Ice House, the Comedy Store and the Improv in Los Angeles. He has performed as a standup in Pittsburgh at the Arcade Comedy Theater, Unplanned Comedy, the Steel City Improv Theater, Greer Cabaret Theater and the Pittsburgh Improv. He has also performed for several local charity events such as Cabaret for a Cause, The GLSEN Awards, and Brewing Up A Cure.

As a writer, Mike has published in a variety of websites, magazines and newspapers. He is a theater and arts critic for 'Burgh Vivant, Pittsburgh's online cultural talk magazine. Buzzelli is also a Moth Grand Slam storyteller and actor, as well as a novelist. *All I Want For Christmas* is his second novel.

CONNECT WITH MIKE:
website: observer-reporter.com/columns/mikebuzzelli
facebook: facebook.com/michael.buzzelli.58
instagram: @michaelbuzzelli
twitter: @MichaelBuzzelli
linkedin: linkedin.com/in/michael-buzzelli-18aa233

www.BOROUGHSPUBLISHINGGROUP.com

If you enjoyed this book, please write a review. Our authors appreciate the feedback, and it helps future readers find books they love. We welcome your comments and invite you to send them to info@boroughspublishinggroup.com. Follow us on Facebook, Twitter and Instagram, and be sure to sign up for our newsletter for surprises and new releases from your favorite authors.

Are you an aspiring writer? Check out www.boroughspublishinggroup.com/submit and see if we can help you make your dreams come true.

www.ingramcontent.com/pod-product-compliance
Lightning Source LLC
Chambersburg PA
CBHW030304130626
46549CB00002B/682